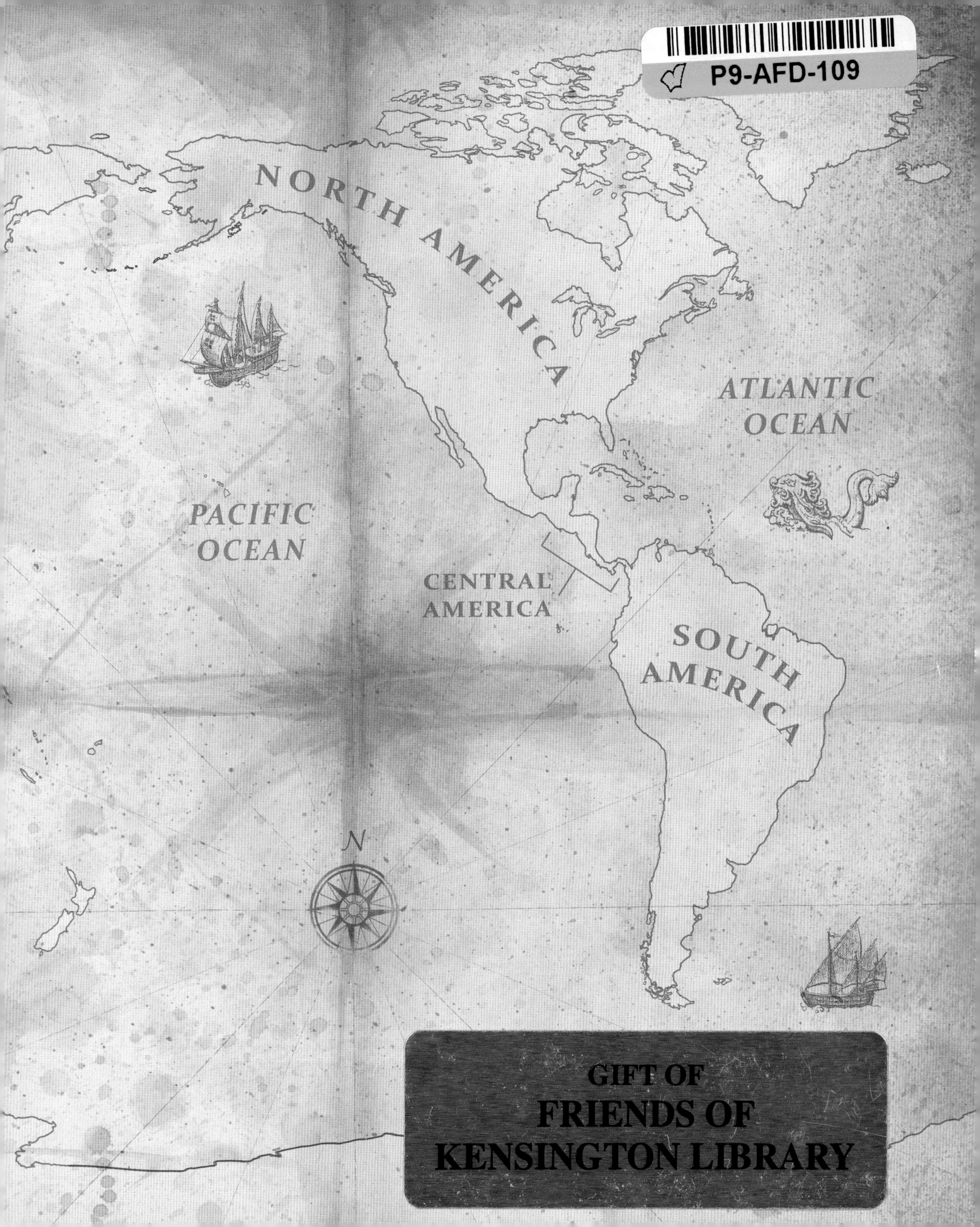
NORTH AMERICA
ATLANTIC OCEAN
PACIFIC OCEAN
CENTRAL AMERICA
SOUTH AMERICA
N

MORTENSEN'S ESCAPADES

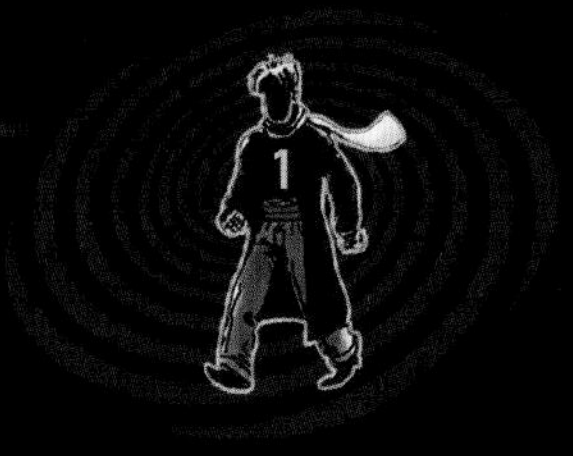

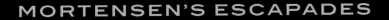

THE MYSTERIOUS MANUSCRIPT

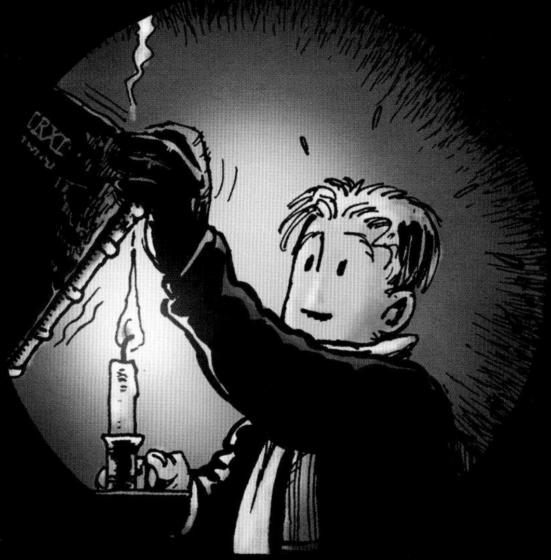

LARS JAKOBSEN

GRAPHIC UNIVERSE™ • MINNEAPOLIS • NEW YORK

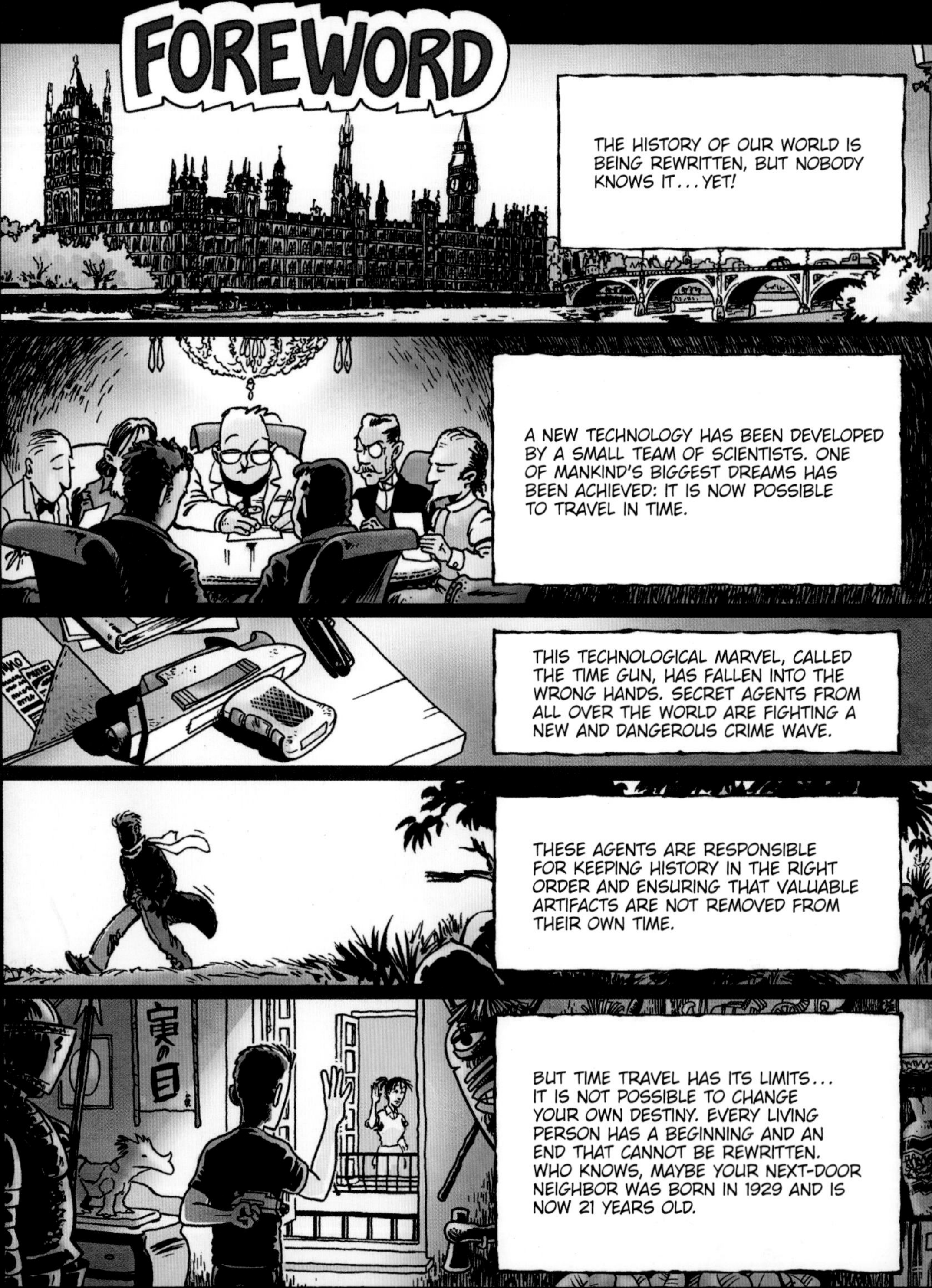
FOREWORD
THE HISTORY OF OUR WORLD IS BEING REWRITTEN, BUT NOBODY KNOWS IT... YET!
A NEW TECHNOLOGY HAS BEEN DEVELOPED BY A SMALL TEAM OF SCIENTISTS. ONE OF MANKIND'S BIGGEST DREAMS HAS BEEN ACHIEVED: IT IS NOW POSSIBLE TO TRAVEL IN TIME.
THIS TECHNOLOGICAL MARVEL, CALLED THE TIME GUN, HAS FALLEN INTO THE WRONG HANDS. SECRET AGENTS FROM ALL OVER THE WORLD ARE FIGHTING A NEW AND DANGEROUS CRIME WAVE.
THESE AGENTS ARE RESPONSIBLE FOR KEEPING HISTORY IN THE RIGHT ORDER AND ENSURING THAT VALUABLE ARTIFACTS ARE NOT REMOVED FROM THEIR OWN TIME.
BUT TIME TRAVEL HAS ITS LIMITS... IT IS NOT POSSIBLE TO CHANGE YOUR OWN DESTINY. EVERY LIVING PERSON HAS A BEGINNING AND AN END THAT CANNOT BE REWRITTEN. WHO KNOWS, MAYBE YOUR NEXT-DOOR NEIGHBOR WAS BORN IN 1929 AND IS NOW 21 YEARS OLD.

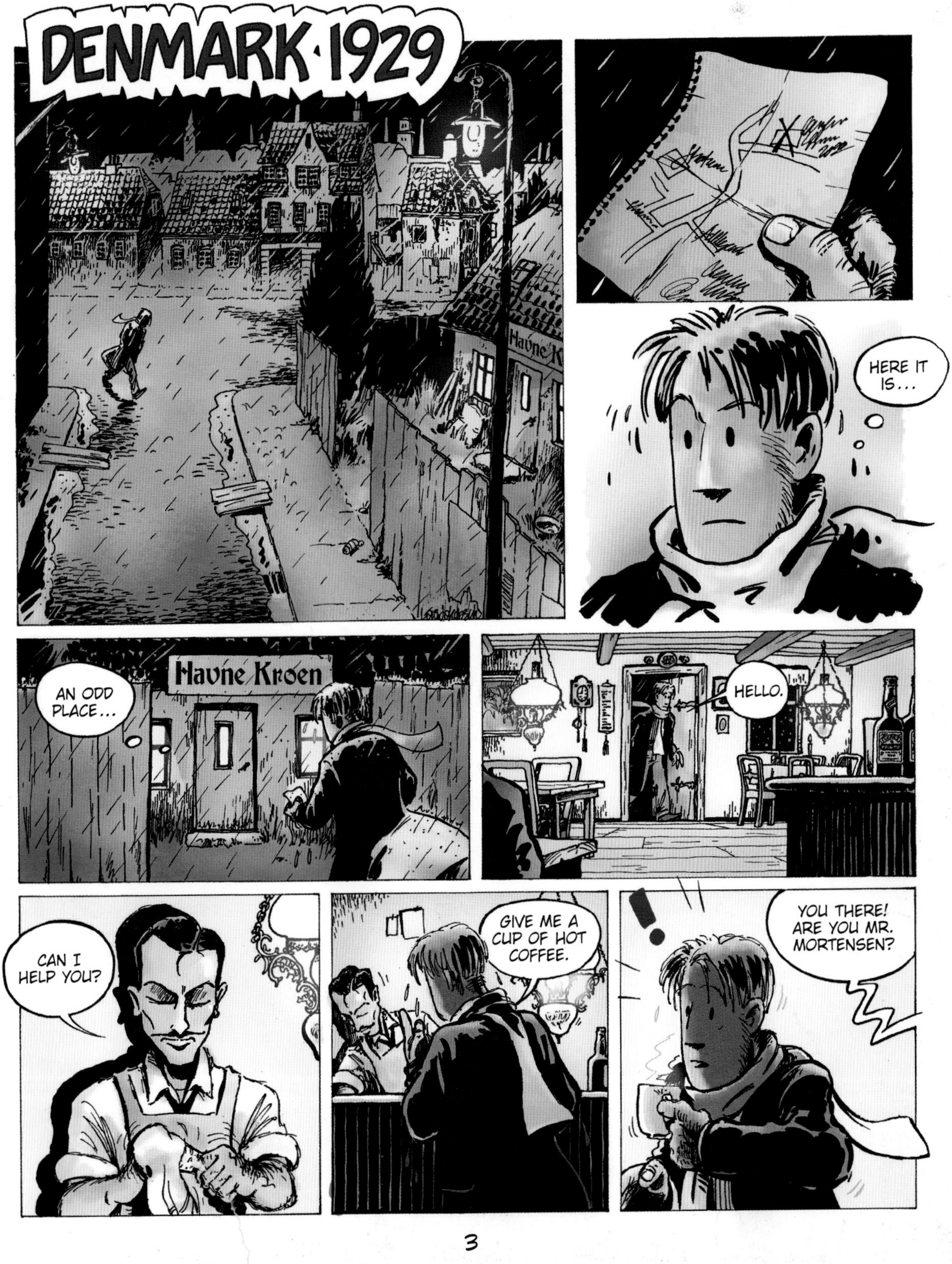
DENMARK · 1929
Havne Kroen
HERE IT IS...
Havne Kroen
AN ODD PLACE...
HELLO.
CAN I HELP YOU?
GIVE ME A CUP OF HOT COFFEE.
!
YOU THERE! ARE YOU MR. MORTENSEN?

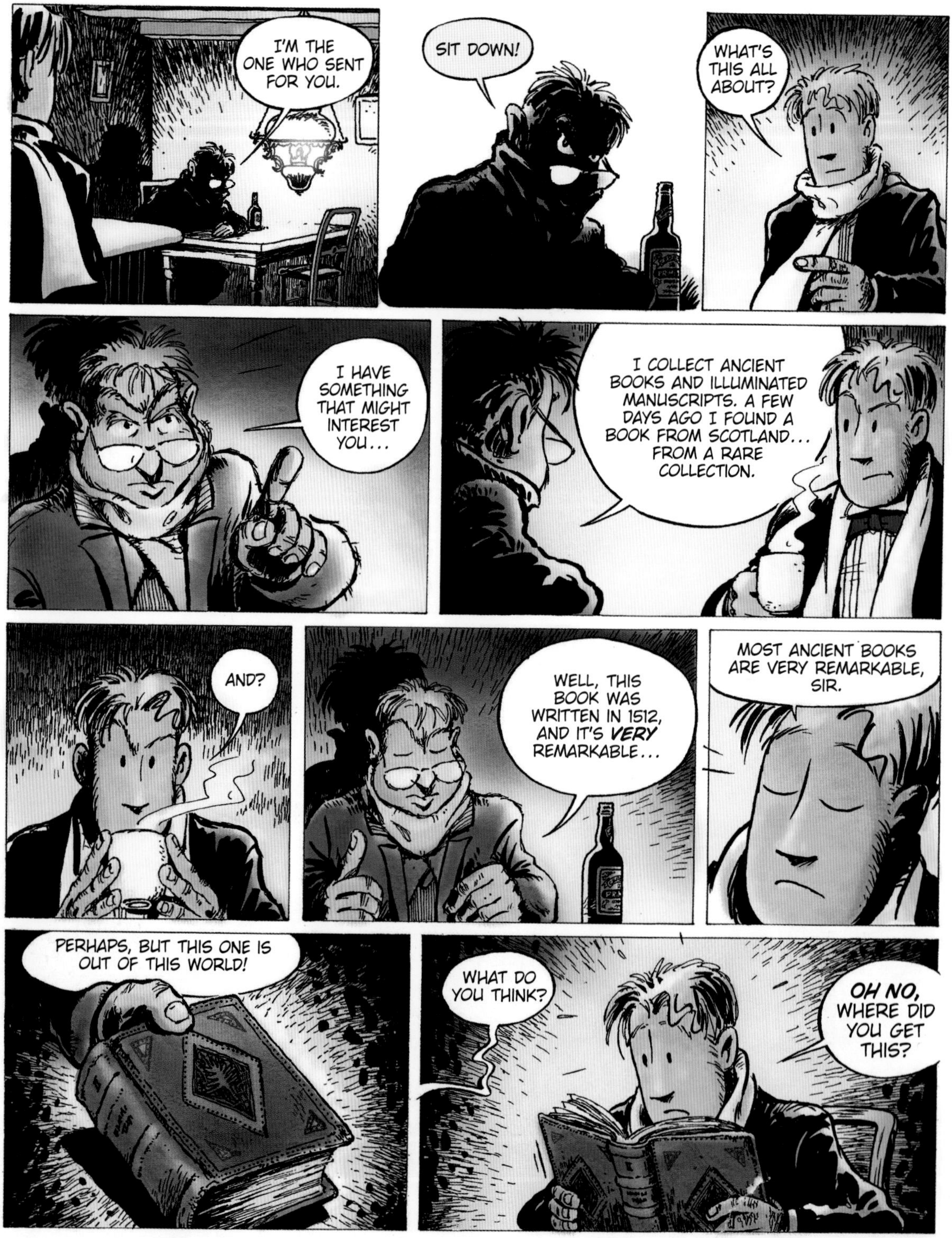
I'M THE ONE WHO SENT FOR YOU.
SIT DOWN!
WHAT'S THIS ALL ABOUT?
I HAVE SOMETHING THAT MIGHT INTEREST YOU...
I COLLECT ANCIENT BOOKS AND ILLUMINATED MANUSCRIPTS. A FEW DAYS AGO I FOUND A BOOK FROM SCOTLAND... FROM A RARE COLLECTION.
AND?
WELL, THIS BOOK WAS WRITTEN IN 1512, AND IT'S ***VERY*** REMARKABLE...
MOST ANCIENT BOOKS ARE VERY REMARKABLE, SIR.
PERHAPS, BUT THIS ONE IS OUT OF THIS WORLD!
WHAT DO YOU THINK?
OH NO, WHERE DID YOU GET THIS?

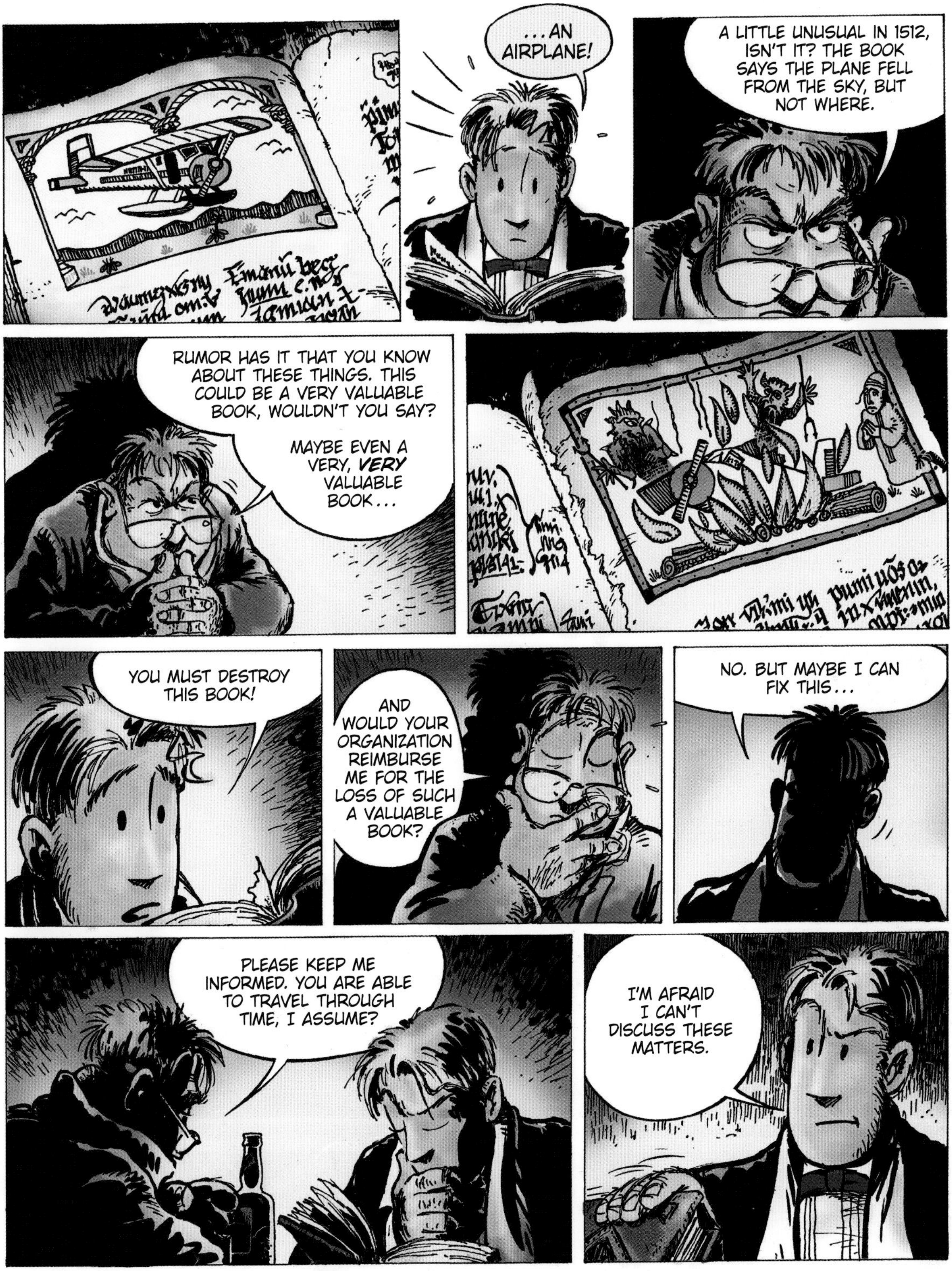
...AN AIRPLANE!
A LITTLE UNUSUAL IN 1512, ISN'T IT? THE BOOK SAYS THE PLANE FELL FROM THE SKY, BUT NOT WHERE.
RUMOR HAS IT THAT YOU KNOW ABOUT THESE THINGS. THIS COULD BE A VERY VALUABLE BOOK, WOULDN'T YOU SAY?
MAYBE EVEN A VERY, **VERY** VALUABLE BOOK...
YOU MUST DESTROY THIS BOOK!
AND WOULD YOUR ORGANIZATION REIMBURSE ME FOR THE LOSS OF SUCH A VALUABLE BOOK?
NO. BUT MAYBE I CAN FIX THIS...
PLEASE KEEP ME INFORMED. YOU ARE ABLE TO TRAVEL THROUGH TIME, I ASSUME?
I'M AFRAID I CAN'T DISCUSS THESE MATTERS.

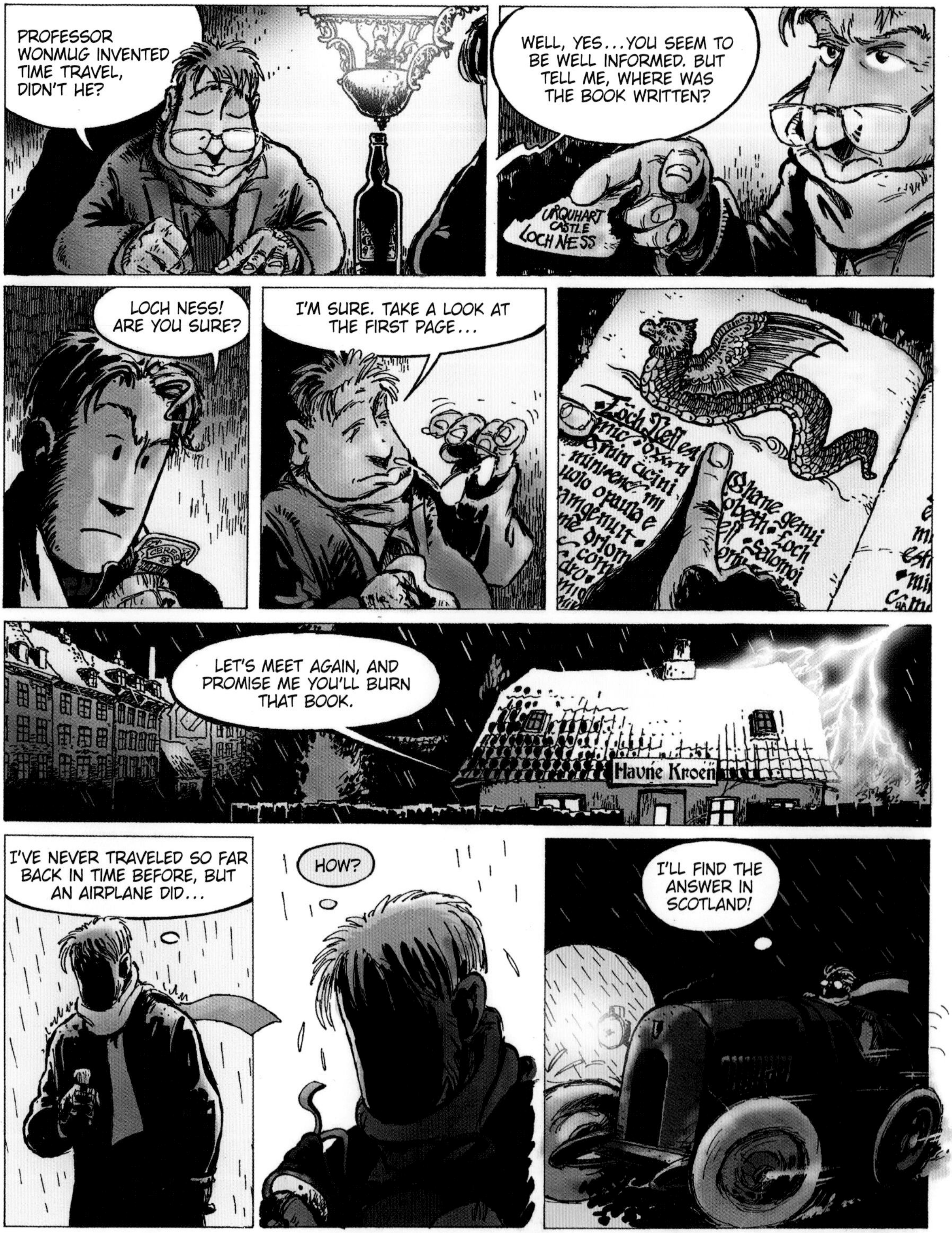
PROFESSOR WONMUG INVENTED TIME TRAVEL, DIDN'T HE?
WELL, YES... YOU SEEM TO BE WELL INFORMED. BUT TELL ME, WHERE WAS THE BOOK WRITTEN?
URQUHART CASTLE LOCH NESS
LOCH NESS! ARE YOU SURE?
I'M SURE. TAKE A LOOK AT THE FIRST PAGE...
LET'S MEET AGAIN, AND PROMISE ME YOU'LL BURN THAT BOOK.
Havne Kroen
I'VE NEVER TRAVELED SO FAR BACK IN TIME BEFORE, BUT AN AIRPLANE DID...
HOW?
I'LL FIND THE ANSWER IN SCOTLAND!

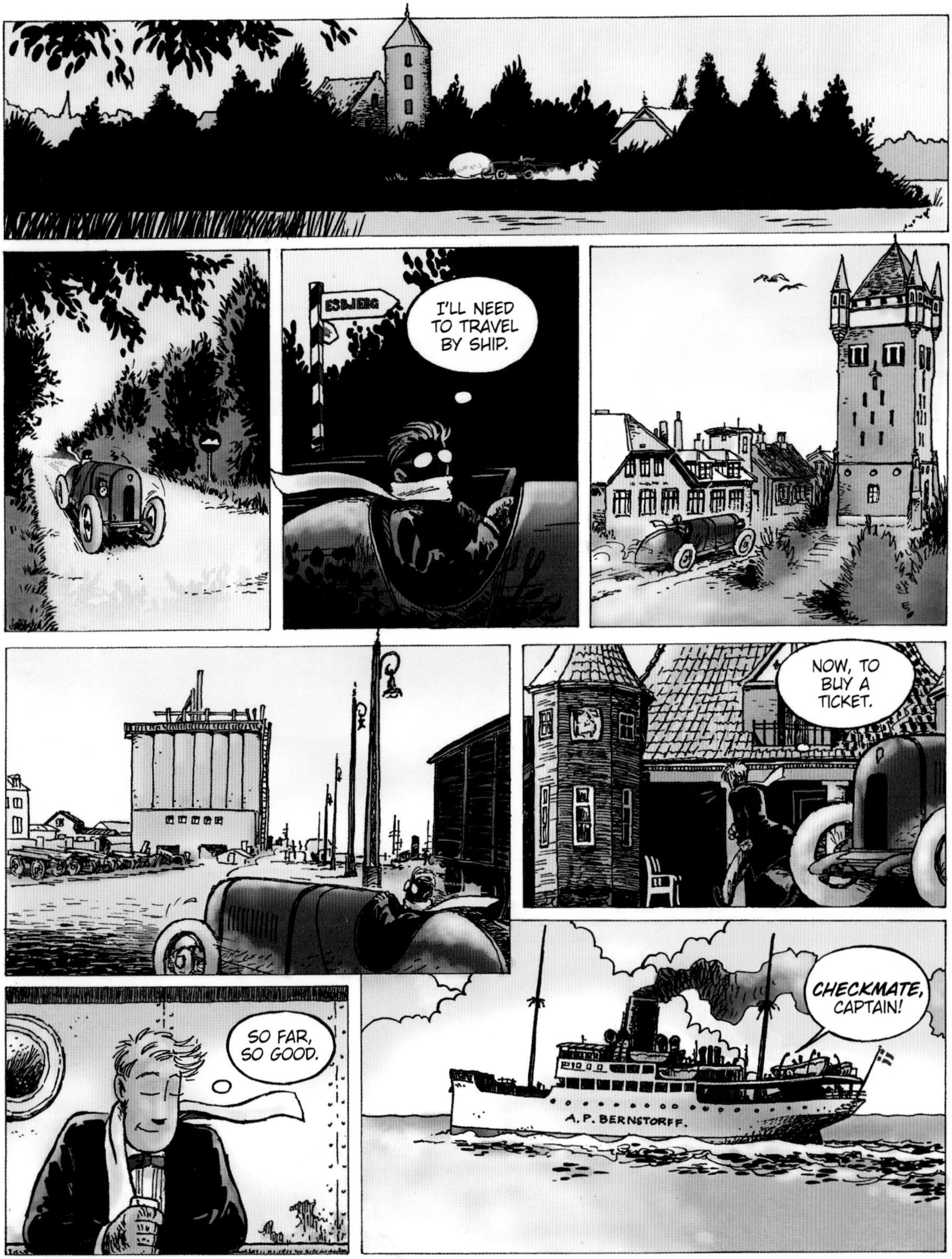
ESBJERG
I'LL NEED TO TRAVEL BY SHIP.
NOW, TO BUY A TICKET.
SO FAR, SO GOOD.
A.P. BERNSTORFF.
CHECKMATE, CAPTAIN!

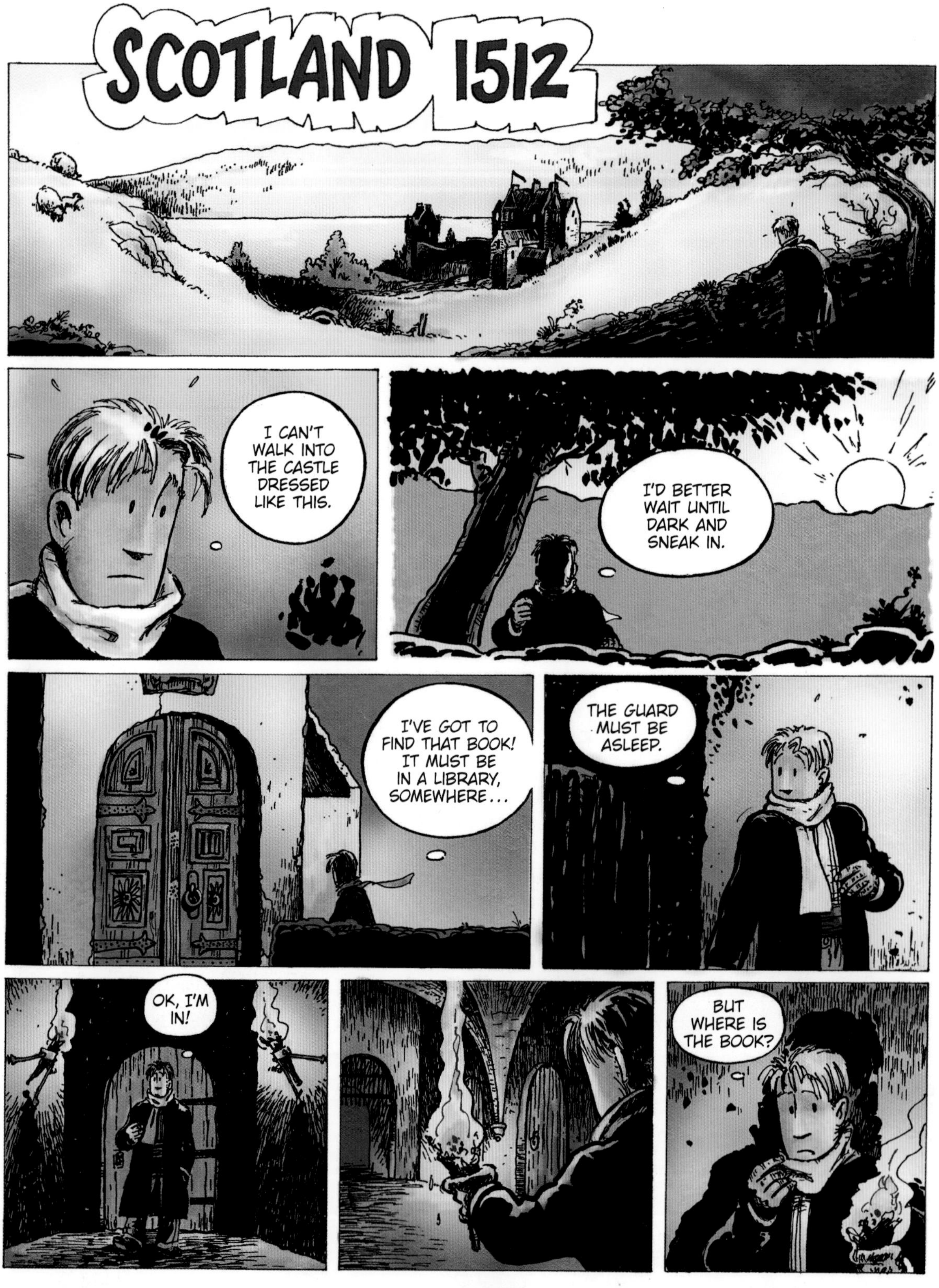
SCOTLAND 1512
I CAN'T WALK INTO THE CASTLE DRESSED LIKE THIS.
I'D BETTER WAIT UNTIL DARK AND SNEAK IN.
I'VE GOT TO FIND THAT BOOK! IT MUST BE IN A LIBRARY, SOMEWHERE...
THE GUARD MUST BE ASLEEP.
OK, I'M IN!
BUT WHERE IS THE BOOK?

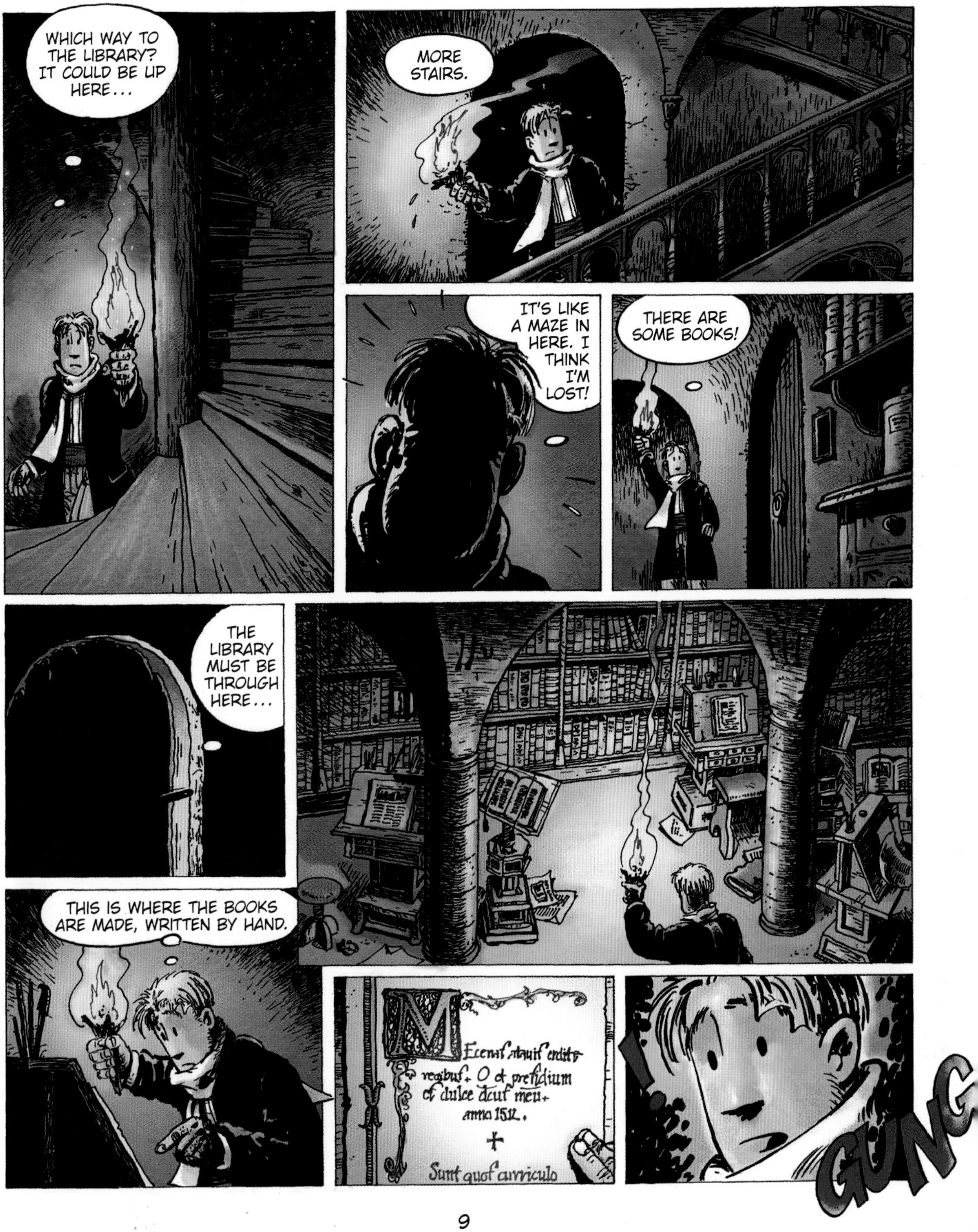
WHICH WAY TO THE LIBRARY? IT COULD BE UP HERE...
MORE STAIRS.
IT'S LIKE A MAZE IN HERE. I THINK I'M LOST!
THERE ARE SOME BOOKS!
THE LIBRARY MUST BE THROUGH HERE...
THIS IS WHERE THE BOOKS ARE MADE, WRITTEN BY HAND.
MEcenaf atauif edite regibuf. O et prefidium et dulce decuf meu. anno 1512.
Sunt quof curriculo
GONG

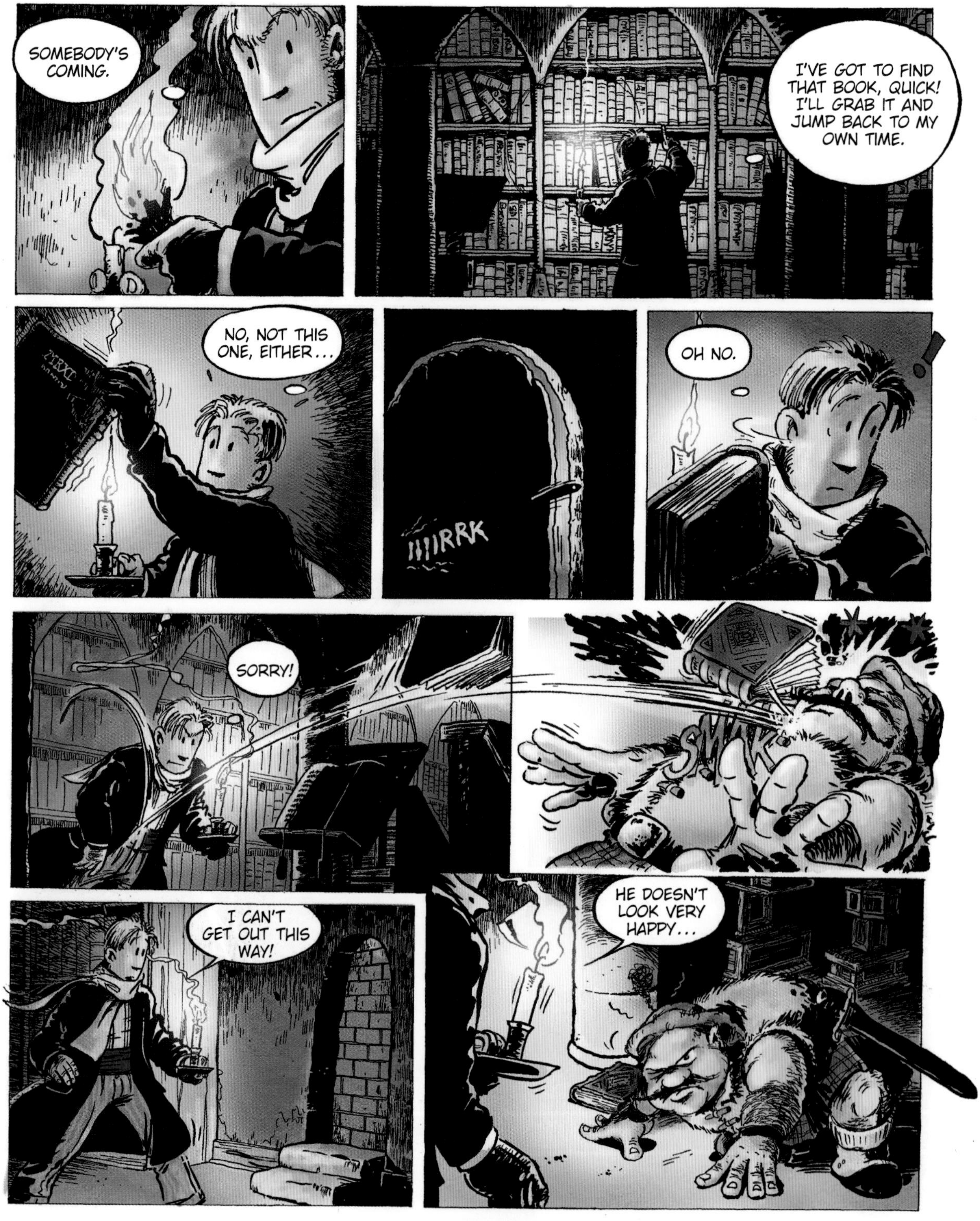
SOMEBODY'S COMING.
I'VE GOT TO FIND THAT BOOK, QUICK! I'LL GRAB IT AND JUMP BACK TO MY OWN TIME.
NO, NOT THIS ONE, EITHER...
IIIIRRK
OH NO.
SORRY!
I CAN'T GET OUT THIS WAY!
HE DOESN'T LOOK VERY HAPPY...

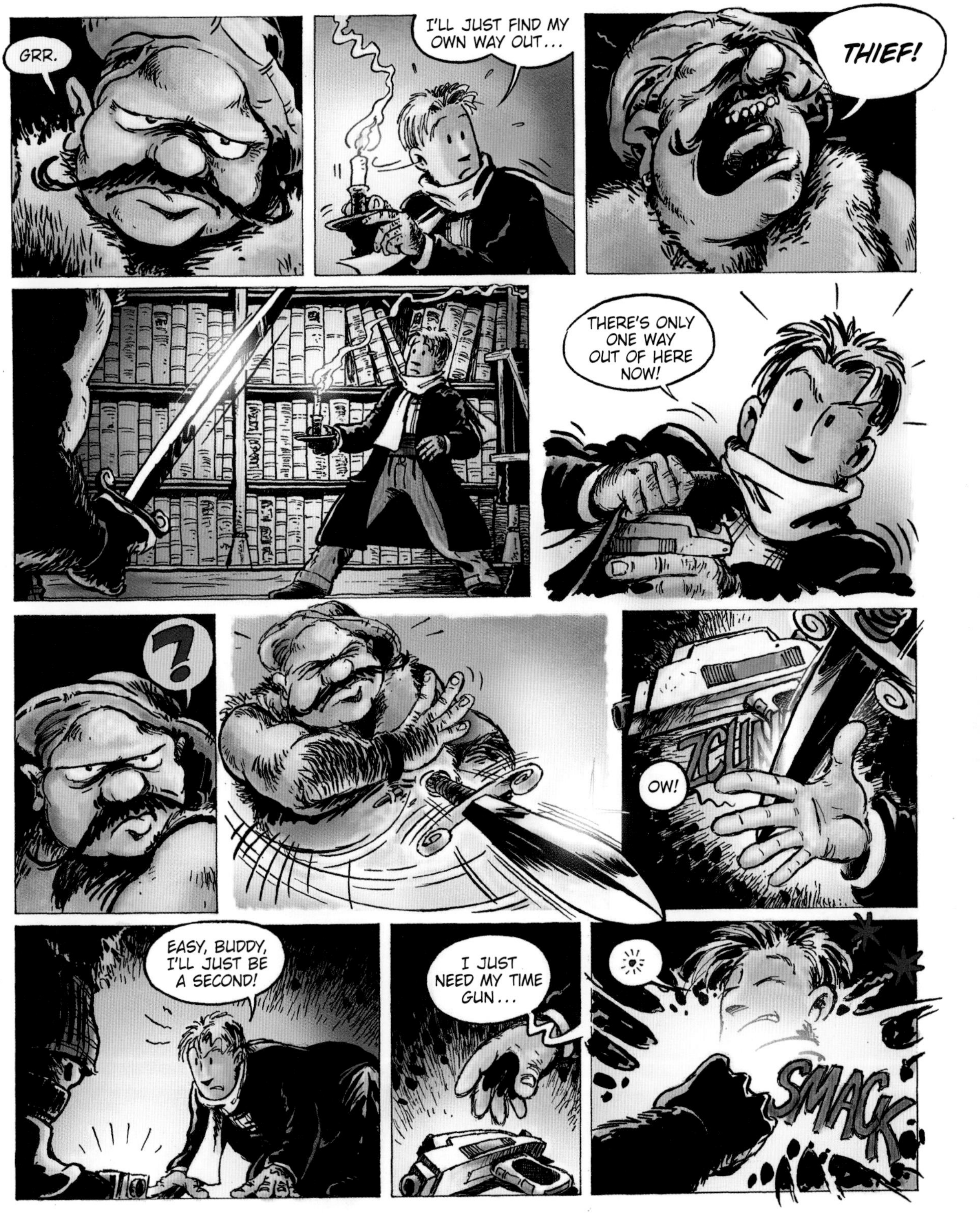
GRR.
I'LL JUST FIND MY OWN WAY OUT...
THIEF!
THERE'S ONLY ONE WAY OUT OF HERE NOW!
?
ZCH
OW!
EASY, BUDDY, I'LL JUST BE A SECOND!
I JUST NEED MY TIME GUN...
SMACK

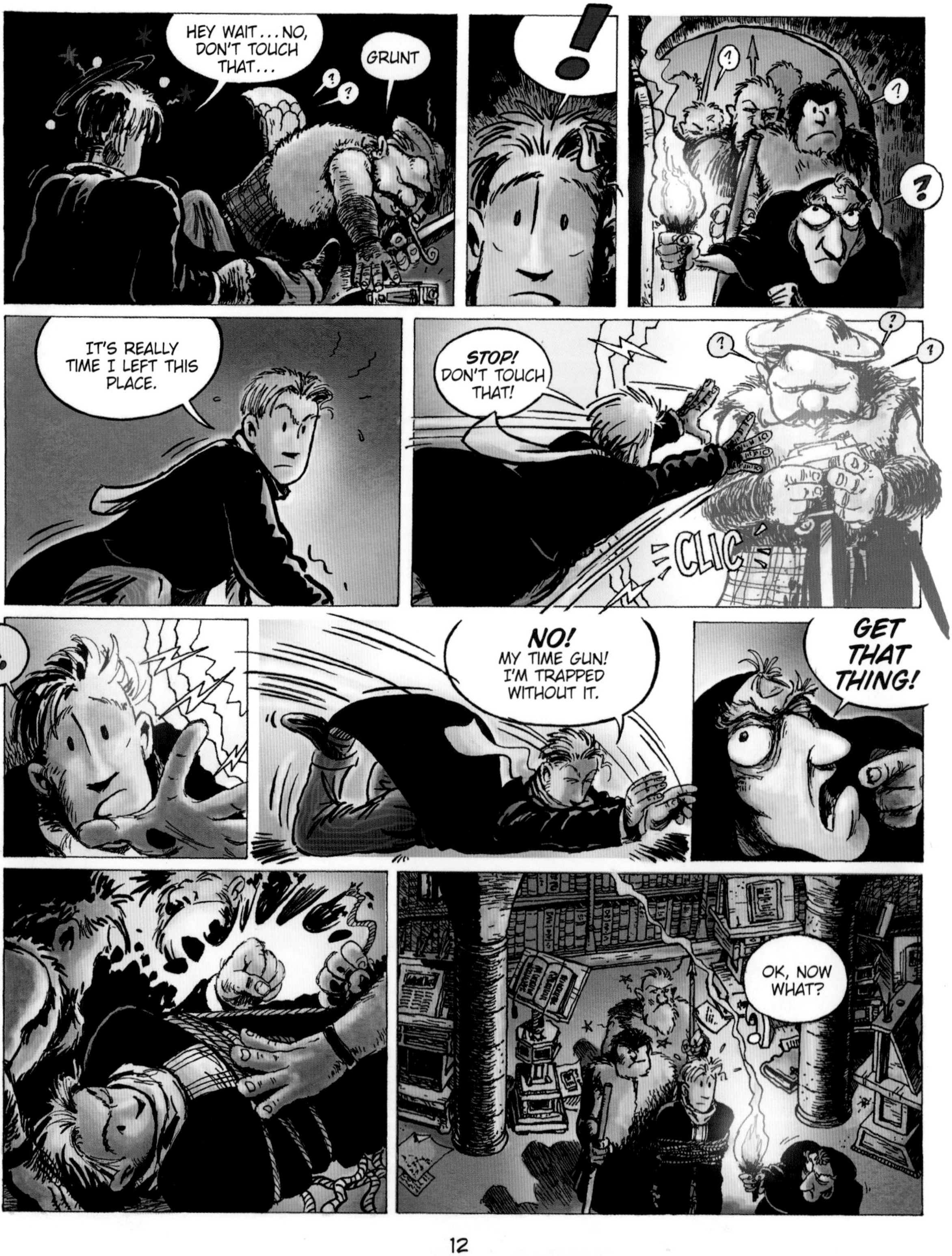
HEY WAIT . . . NO, DON'T TOUCH THAT . . .
GRUNT
?
?
!
?
?
?
IT'S REALLY TIME I LEFT THIS PLACE.
STOP! DON'T TOUCH THAT!
?
?
?
CLIC
!
NO! MY TIME GUN! I'M TRAPPED WITHOUT IT.
GET THAT THING!
OK, NOW WHAT?

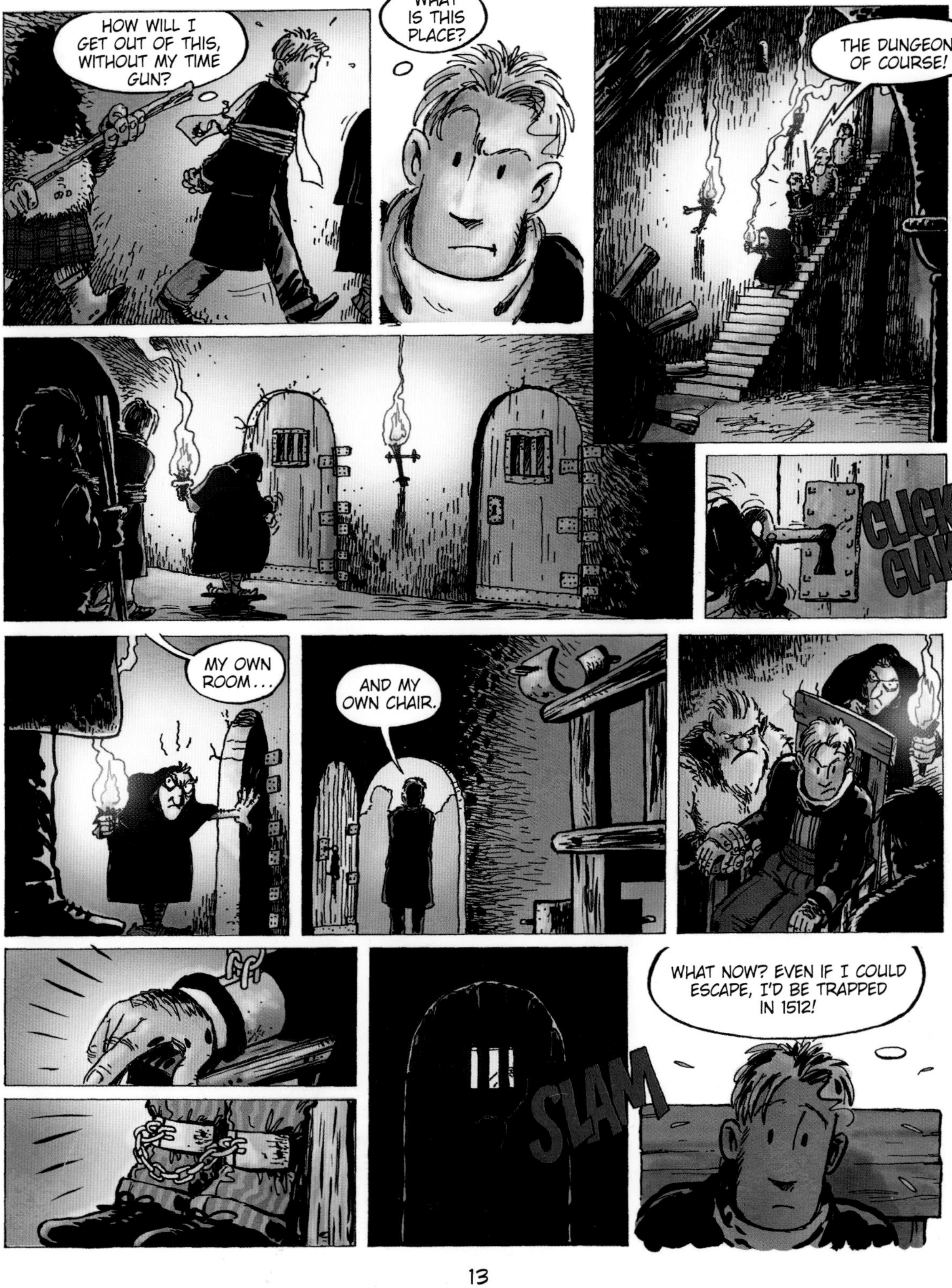
HOW WILL I GET OUT OF THIS, WITHOUT MY TIME GUN?
WHAT IS THIS PLACE?
THE DUNGEON, OF COURSE!
CLICK
CLAK
MY OWN ROOM...
AND MY OWN CHAIR.
SLAM
WHAT NOW? EVEN IF I COULD ESCAPE, I'D BE TRAPPED IN 1512!

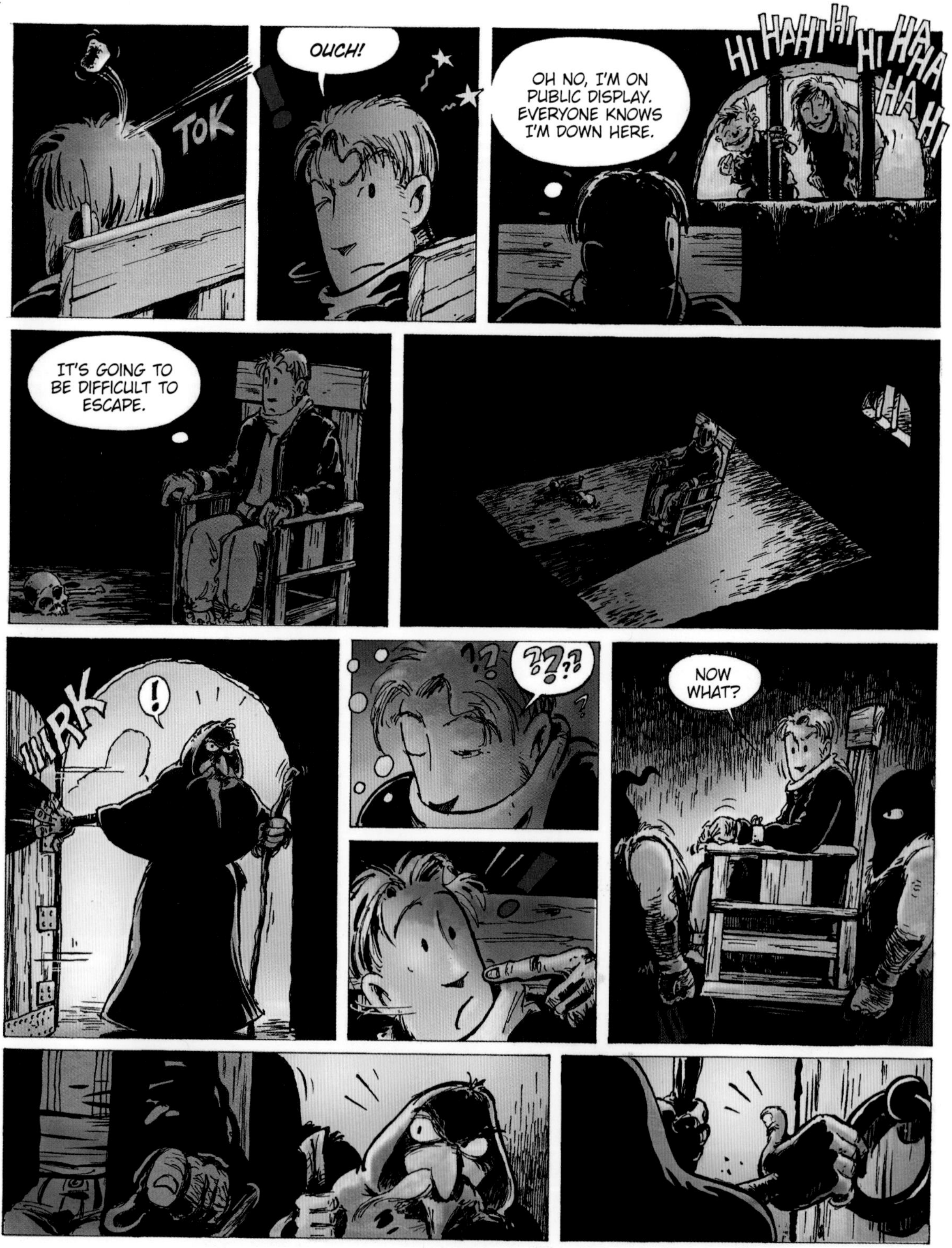
TOK
OUCH!
OH NO, I'M ON PUBLIC DISPLAY. EVERYONE KNOWS I'M DOWN HERE.
HI HA HI HI HI HA HA HA HA HA HI
IT'S GOING TO BE DIFFICULT TO ESCAPE.
RK
!
???
NOW WHAT?

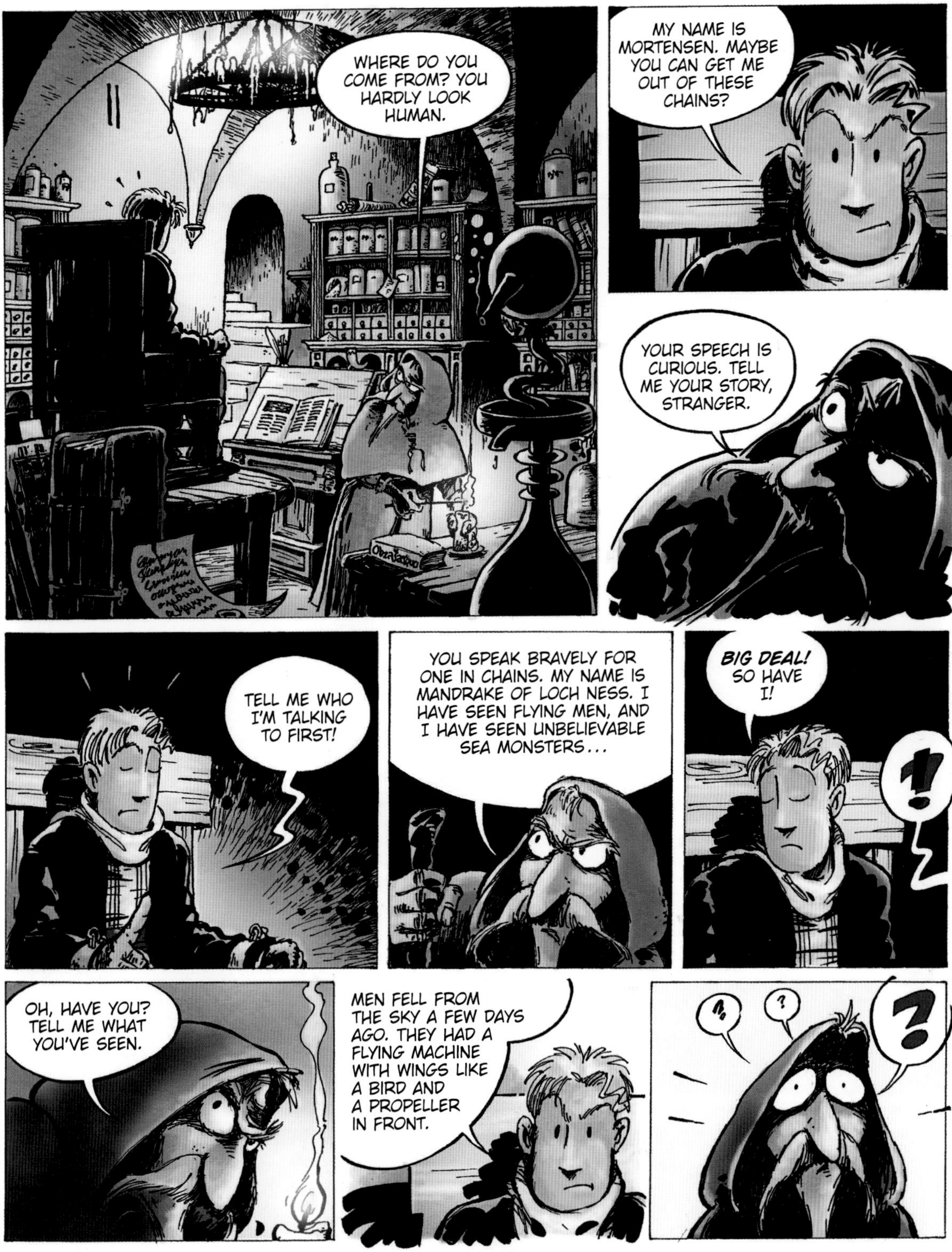
WHERE DO YOU COME FROM? YOU HARDLY LOOK HUMAN.
MY NAME IS MORTENSEN. MAYBE YOU CAN GET ME OUT OF THESE CHAINS?
YOUR SPEECH IS CURIOUS. TELL ME YOUR STORY, STRANGER.
TELL ME WHO I'M TALKING TO FIRST!
YOU SPEAK BRAVELY FOR ONE IN CHAINS. MY NAME IS MANDRAKE OF LOCH NESS. I HAVE SEEN FLYING MEN, AND I HAVE SEEN UNBELIEVABLE SEA MONSTERS...
BIG DEAL! SO HAVE I!
!
OH, HAVE YOU? TELL ME WHAT YOU'VE SEEN.
MEN FELL FROM THE SKY A FEW DAYS AGO. THEY HAD A FLYING MACHINE WITH WINGS LIKE A BIRD AND A PROPELLER IN FRONT.
?
?
?

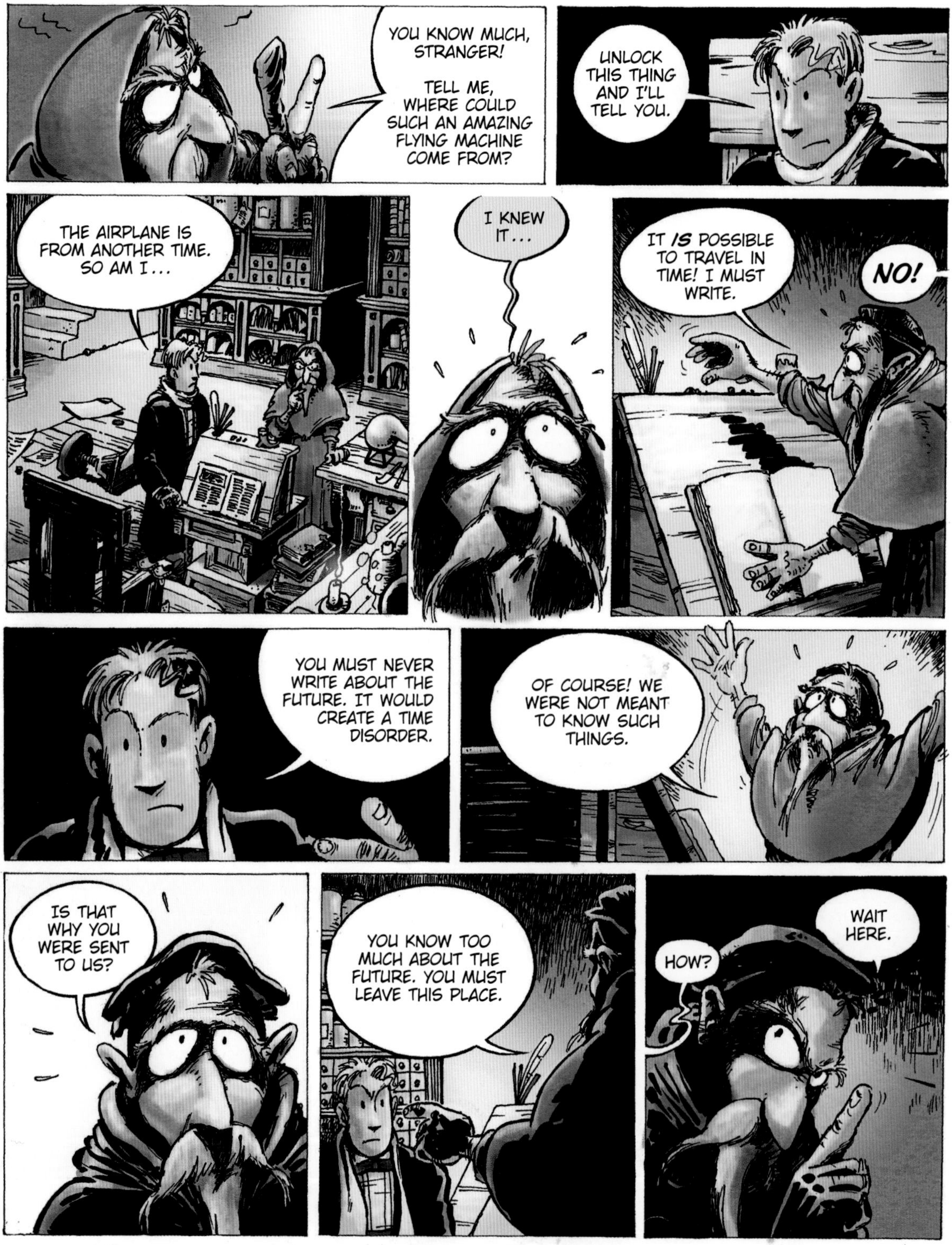

YOU KNOW MUCH, STRANGER!
TELL ME, WHERE COULD SUCH AN AMAZING FLYING MACHINE COME FROM?
UNLOCK THIS THING AND I'LL TELL YOU.
THE AIRPLANE IS FROM ANOTHER TIME. SO AM I...
I KNEW IT...
IT *IS* POSSIBLE TO TRAVEL IN TIME! I MUST WRITE.
NO!
YOU MUST NEVER WRITE ABOUT THE FUTURE. IT WOULD CREATE A TIME DISORDER.
OF COURSE! WE WERE NOT MEANT TO KNOW SUCH THINGS.
IS THAT WHY YOU WERE SENT TO US?
YOU KNOW TOO MUCH ABOUT THE FUTURE. YOU MUST LEAVE THIS PLACE.
HOW?
WAIT HERE.

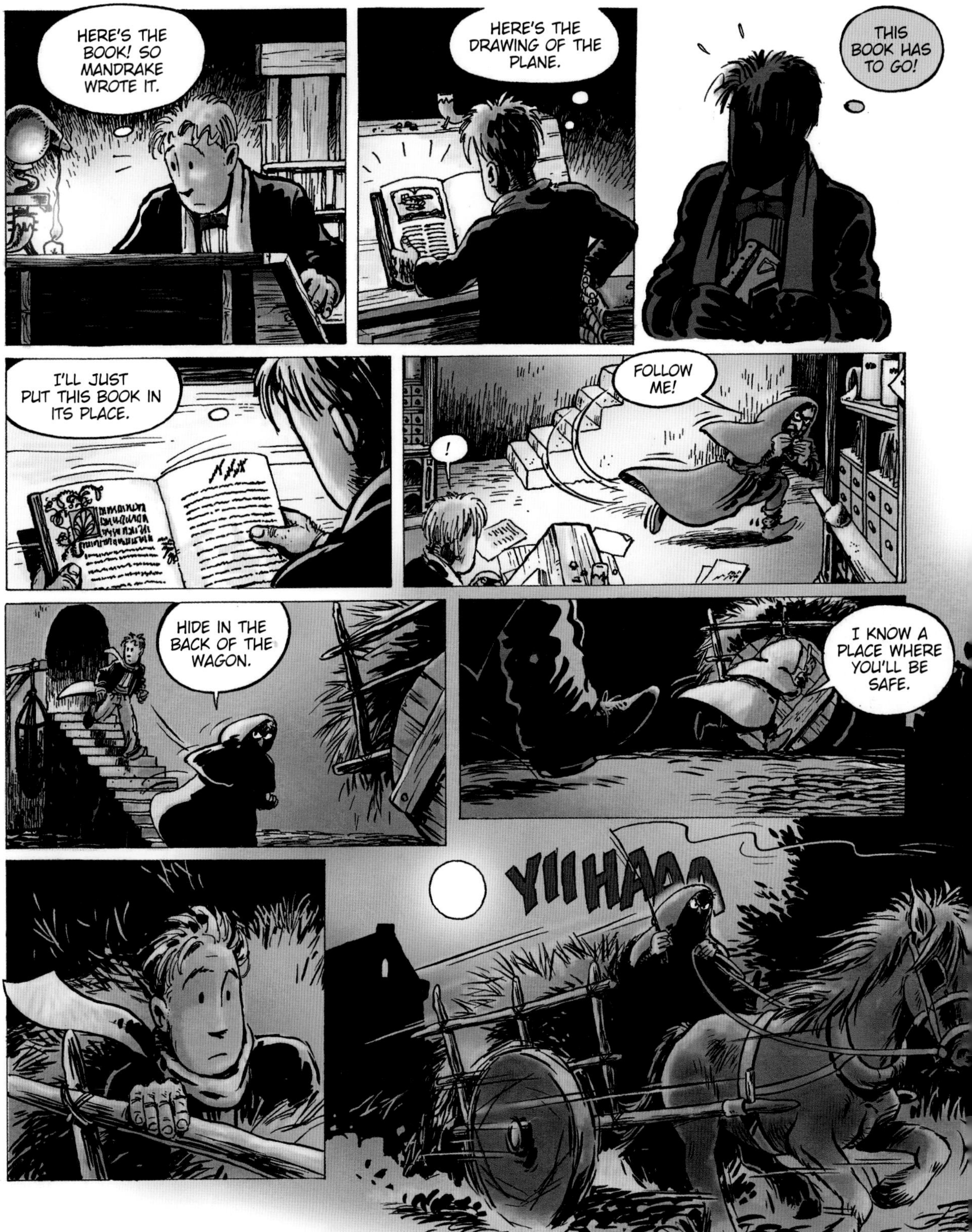
HERE'S THE BOOK! SO MANDRAKE WROTE IT.
HERE'S THE DRAWING OF THE PLANE.
THIS BOOK HAS TO GO!
I'LL JUST PUT THIS BOOK IN ITS PLACE.
FOLLOW ME!
!
HIDE IN THE BACK OF THE WAGON.
I KNOW A PLACE WHERE YOU'LL BE SAFE.
YII HAAA

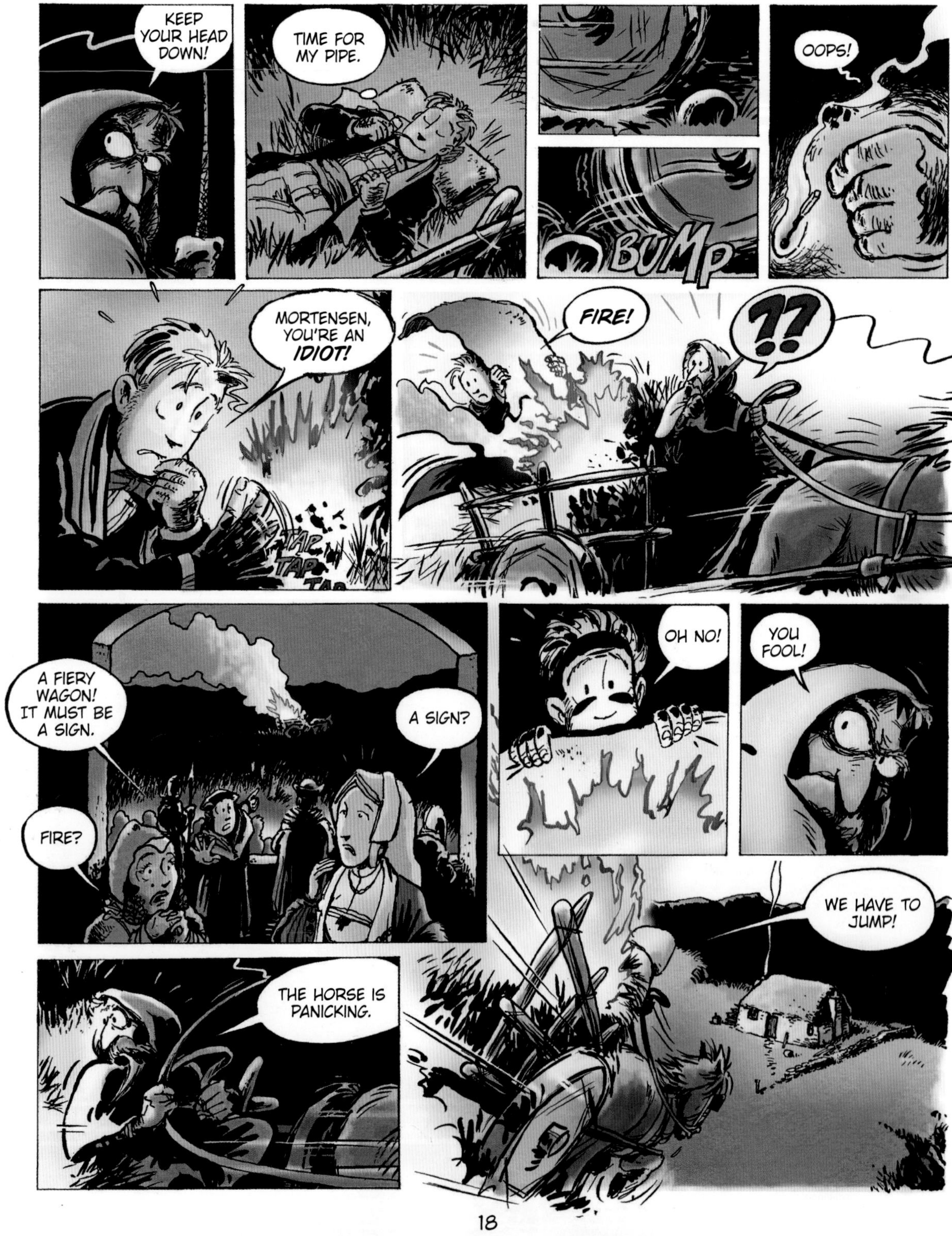
KEEP YOUR HEAD DOWN!
TIME FOR MY PIPE.
BUMP
OOPS!
MORTENSEN, YOU'RE AN IDIOT!
TAP TAP TAP
FIRE!
??
A FIERY WAGON! IT MUST BE A SIGN.
A SIGN?
FIRE?
OH NO!
YOU FOOL!
THE HORSE IS PANICKING.
WE HAVE TO JUMP!

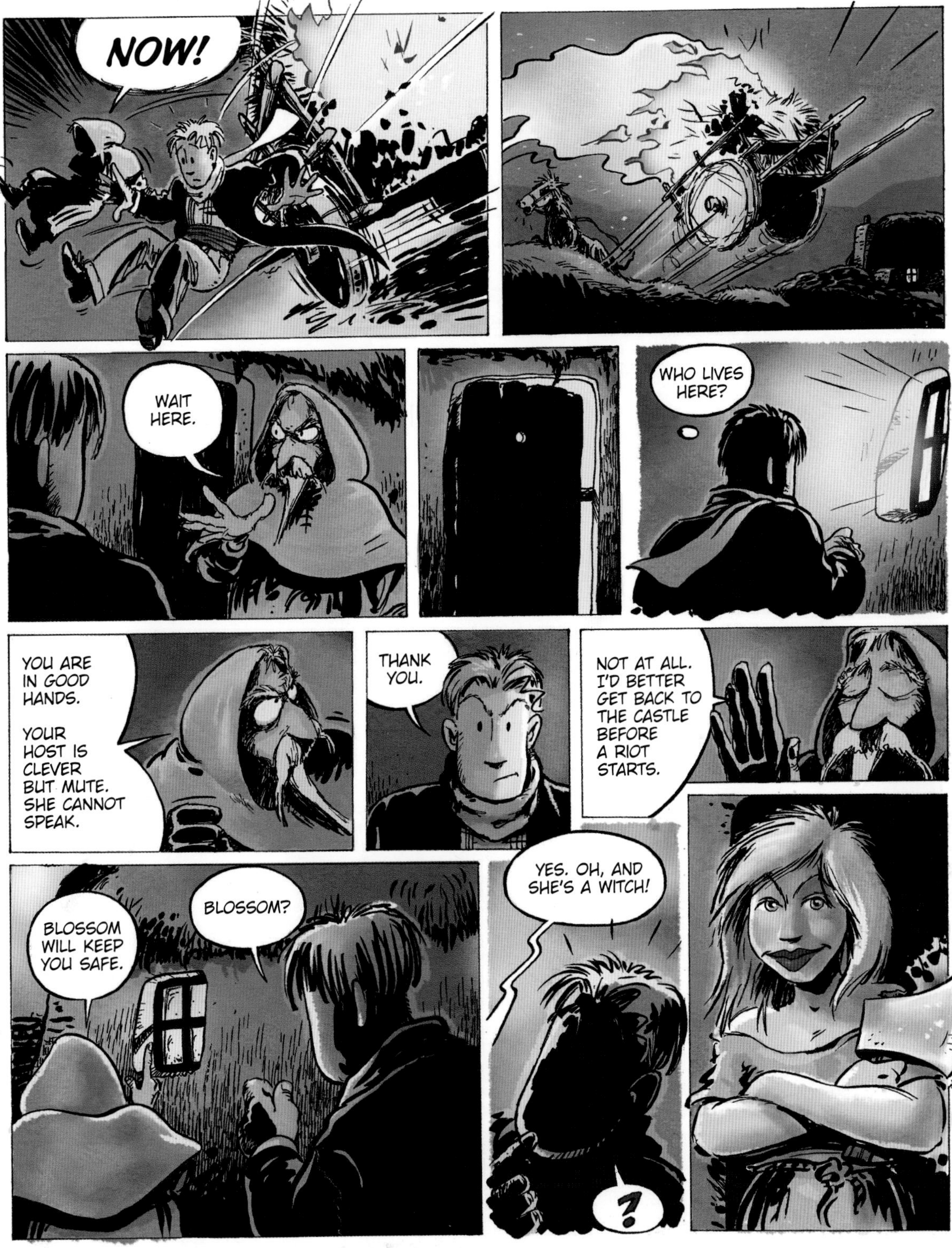
NOW!
WAIT HERE.
WHO LIVES HERE?
YOU ARE IN GOOD HANDS.
YOUR HOST IS CLEVER BUT MUTE. SHE CANNOT SPEAK.
THANK YOU.
NOT AT ALL. I'D BETTER GET BACK TO THE CASTLE BEFORE A RIOT STARTS.
BLOSSOM WILL KEEP YOU SAFE.
BLOSSOM?
YES. OH, AND SHE'S A WITCH!
?

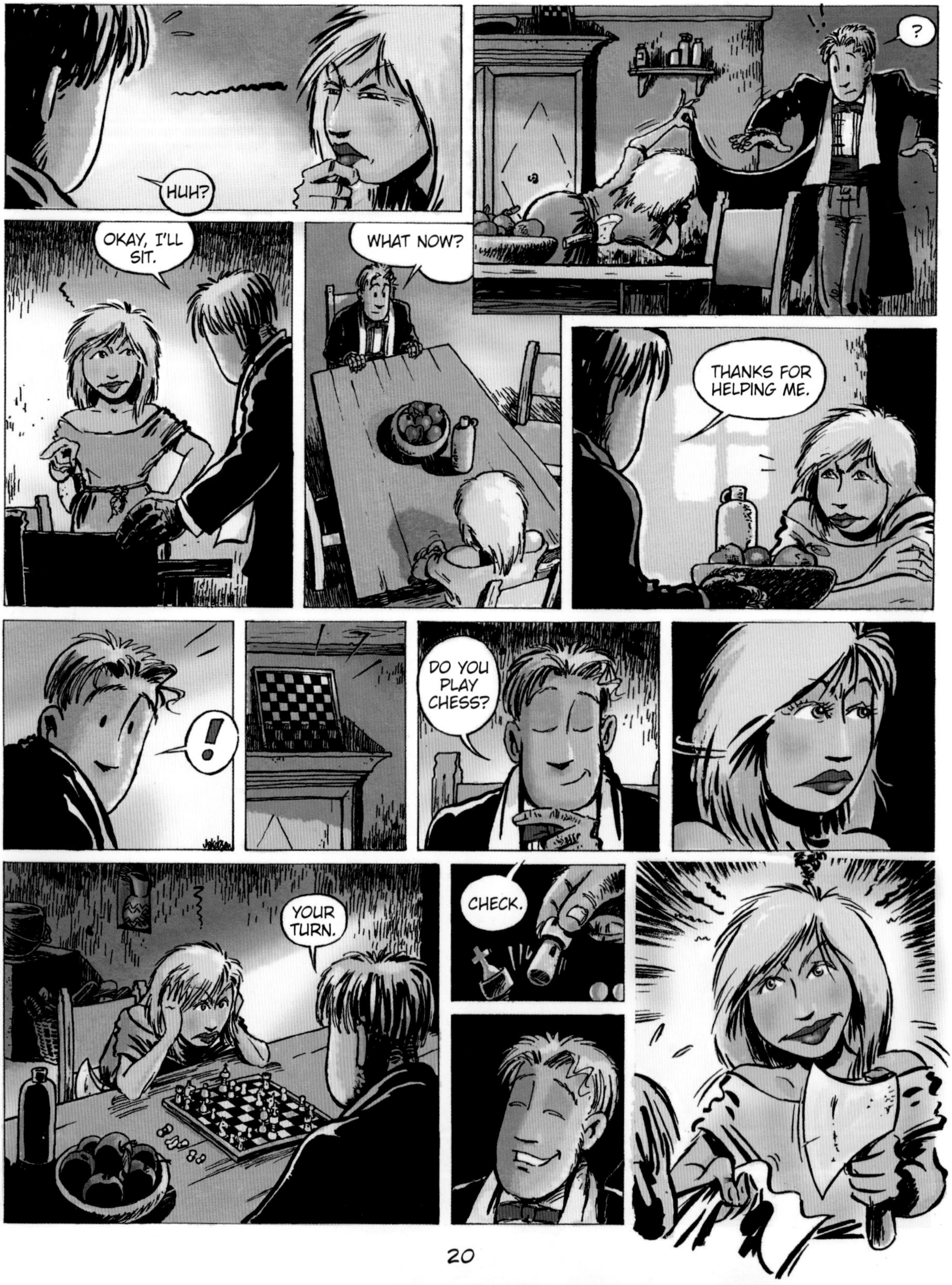
HUH?
?
OKAY, I'LL SIT.
WHAT NOW?
THANKS FOR HELPING ME.
!
DO YOU PLAY CHESS?
YOUR TURN.
CHECK.

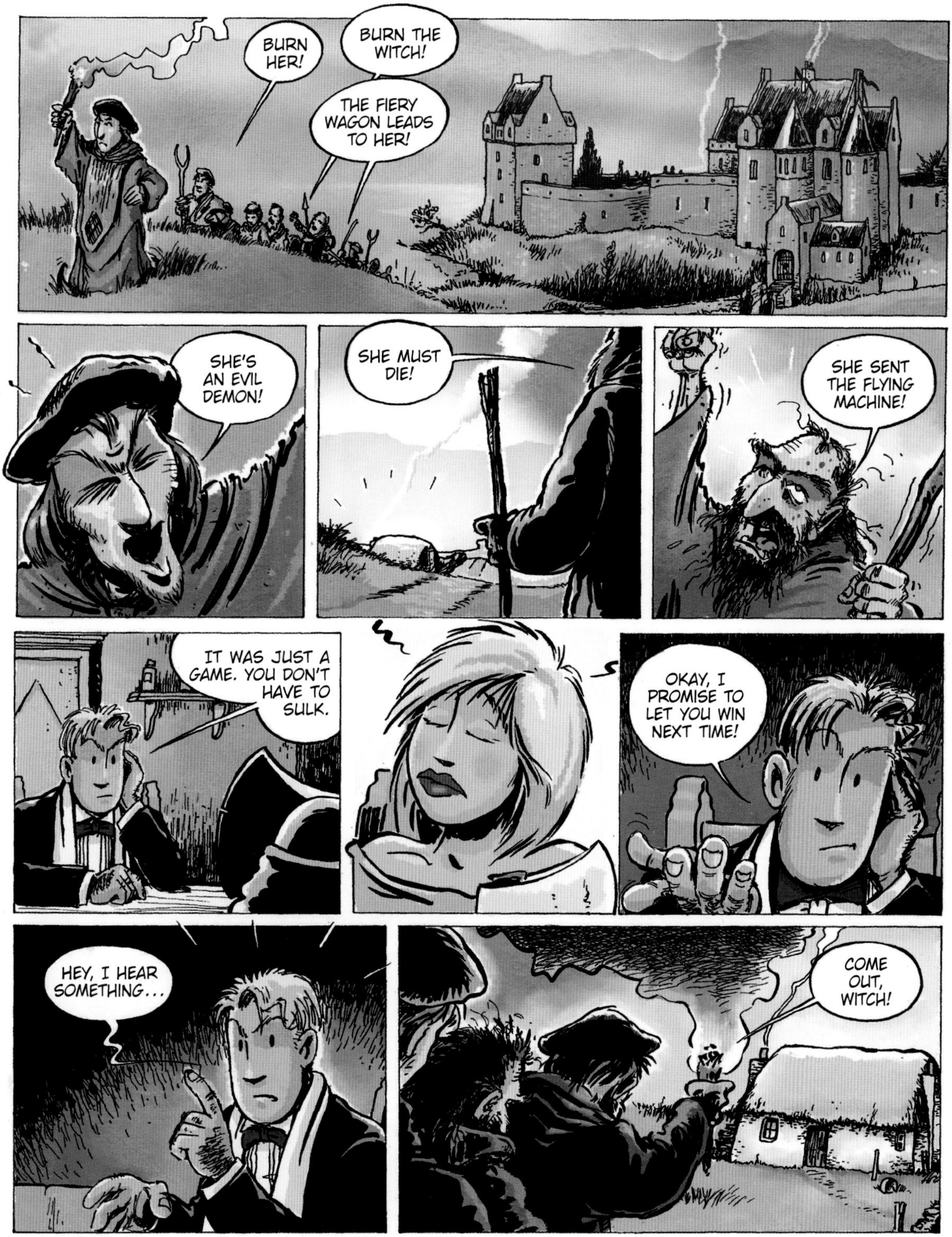
BURN HER!
BURN THE WITCH!
THE FIERY WAGON LEADS TO HER!
SHE'S AN EVIL DEMON!
SHE MUST DIE!
SHE SENT THE FLYING MACHINE!
IT WAS JUST A GAME. YOU DON'T HAVE TO SULK.
OKAY, I PROMISE TO LET YOU WIN NEXT TIME!
HEY, I HEAR SOMETHING...
COME OUT, WITCH!

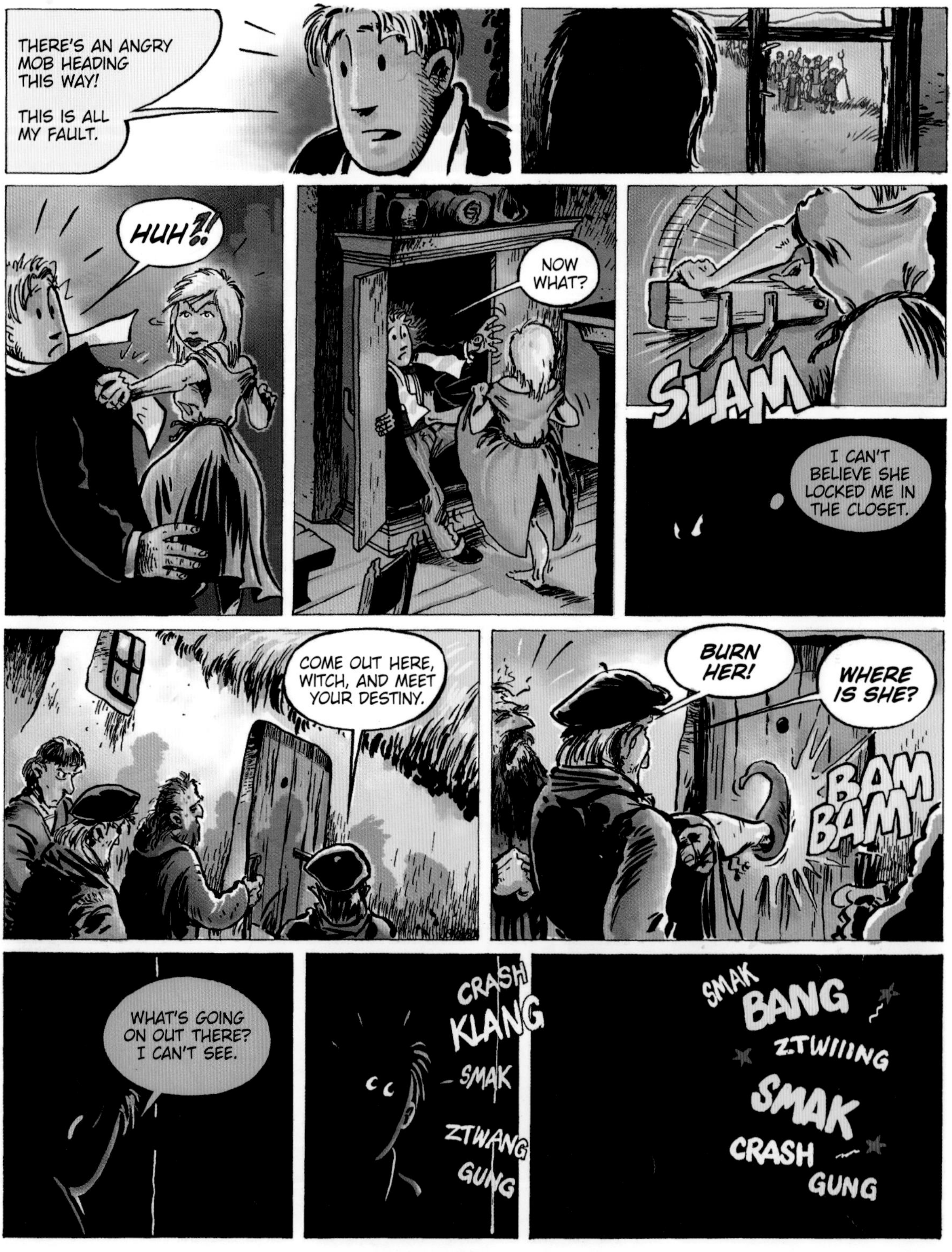
THERE'S AN ANGRY MOB HEADING THIS WAY!
THIS IS ALL MY FAULT.
HUH?!
NOW WHAT?
SLAM
I CAN'T BELIEVE SHE LOCKED ME IN THE CLOSET.
COME OUT HERE, WITCH, AND MEET YOUR DESTINY.
BURN HER!
WHERE IS SHE?
BAM BAM
WHAT'S GOING ON OUT THERE? I CAN'T SEE.
CRASH
KLANG
SMAK
ZTWANG
GUNG
SMAK
BANG
ZTWIIING
SMAK
CRASH
GUNG

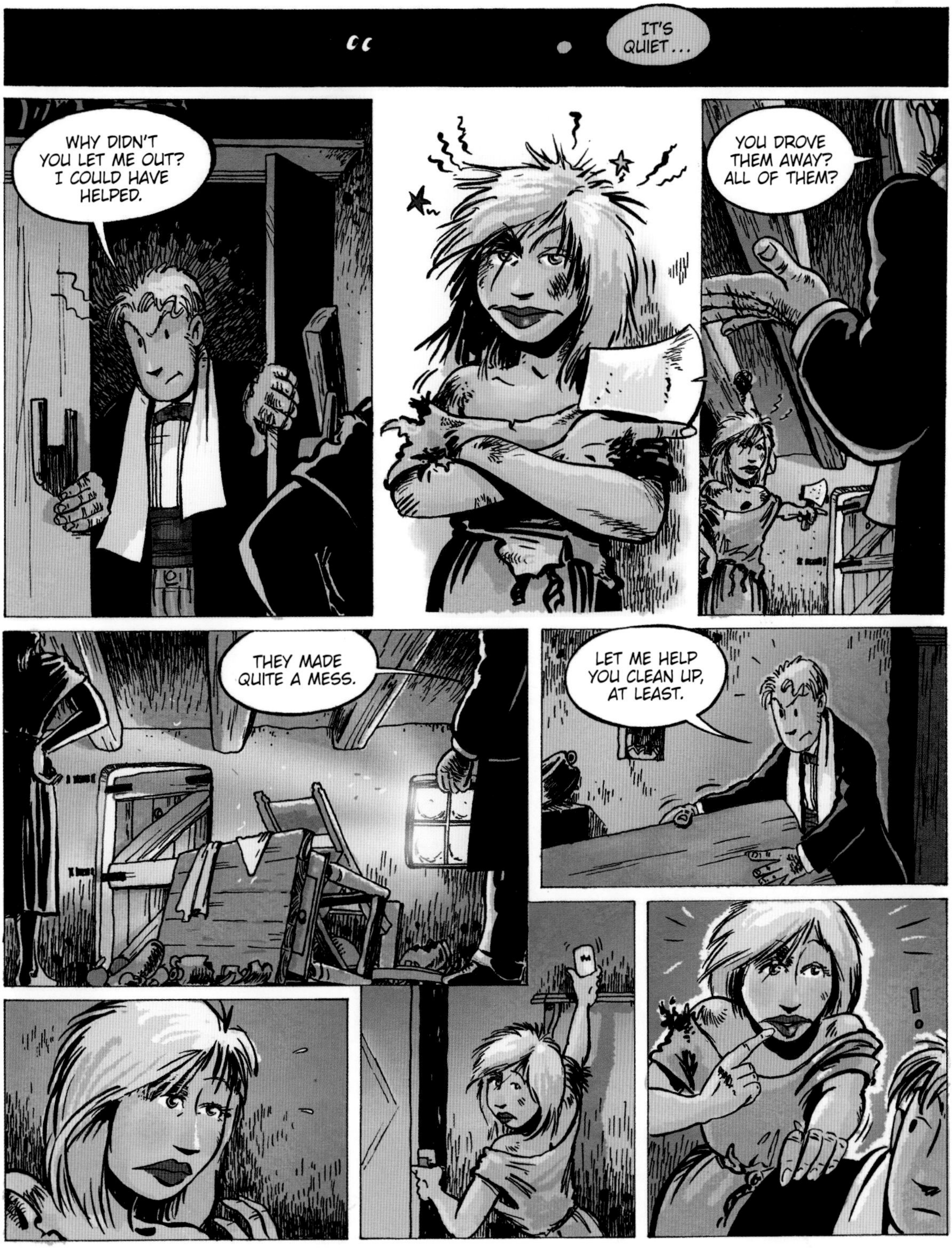
IT'S QUIET...
WHY DIDN'T YOU LET ME OUT? I COULD HAVE HELPED.
YOU DROVE THEM AWAY? ALL OF THEM?
THEY MADE QUITE A MESS.
LET ME HELP YOU CLEAN UP, AT LEAST.
!

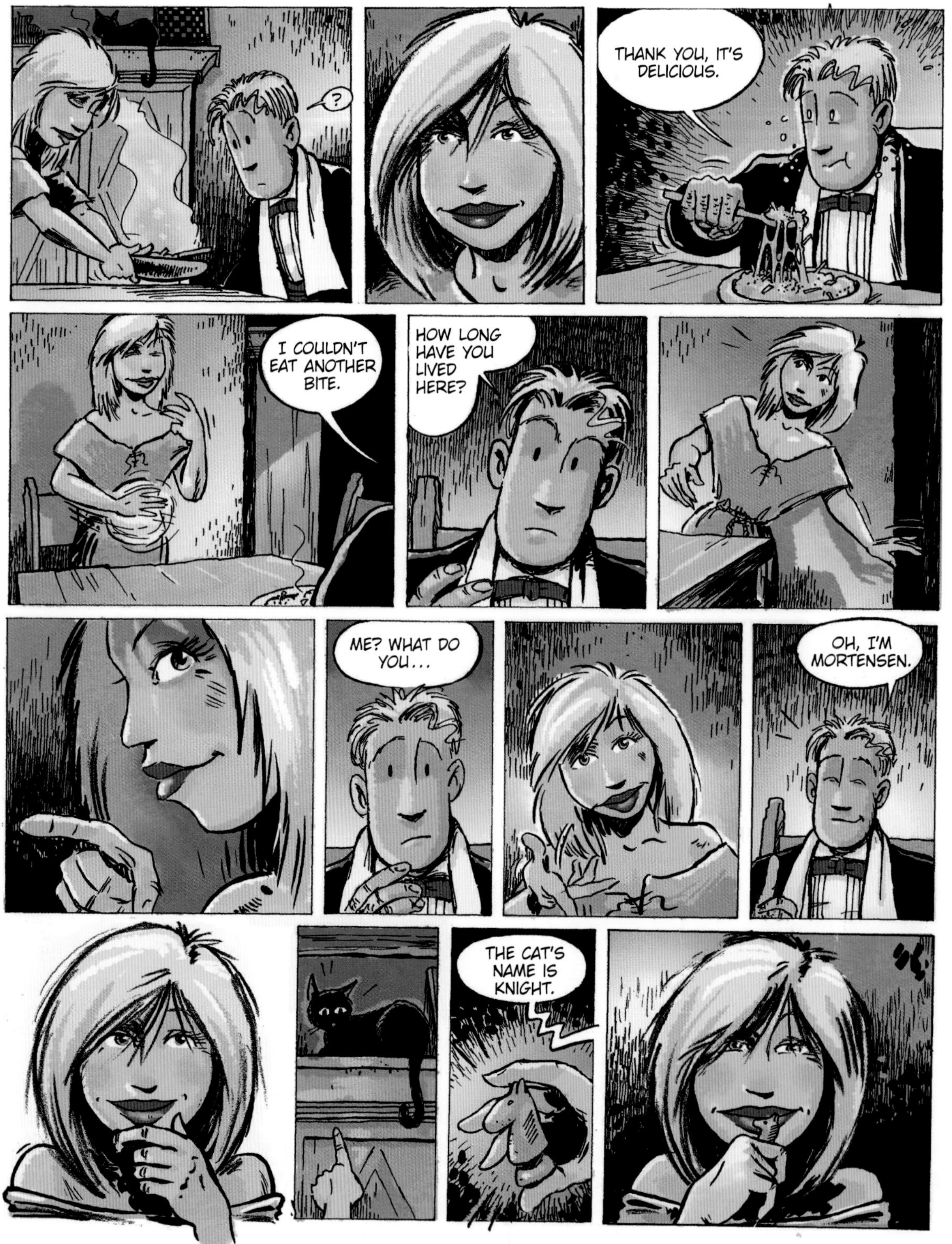
?
THANK YOU, IT'S DELICIOUS.
I COULDN'T EAT ANOTHER BITE.
HOW LONG HAVE YOU LIVED HERE?
ME? WHAT DO YOU...
OH, I'M MORTENSEN.
THE CAT'S NAME IS KNIGHT.

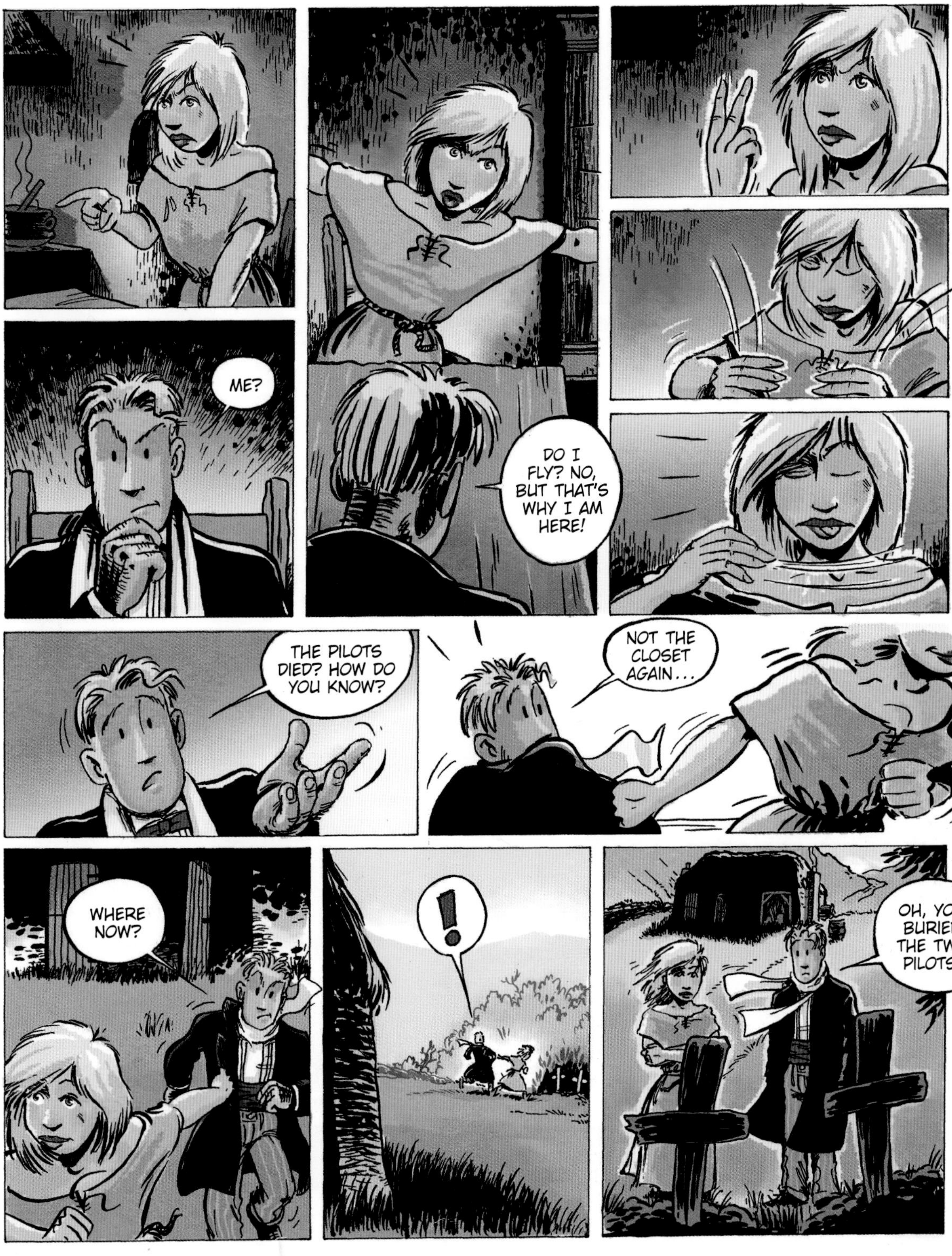

ME?
DO I FLY? NO, BUT THAT'S WHY I AM HERE!
THE PILOTS DIED? HOW DO YOU KNOW?
NOT THE CLOSET AGAIN...
WHERE NOW?
!
OH, YOU BURIED THE TWO PILOTS.

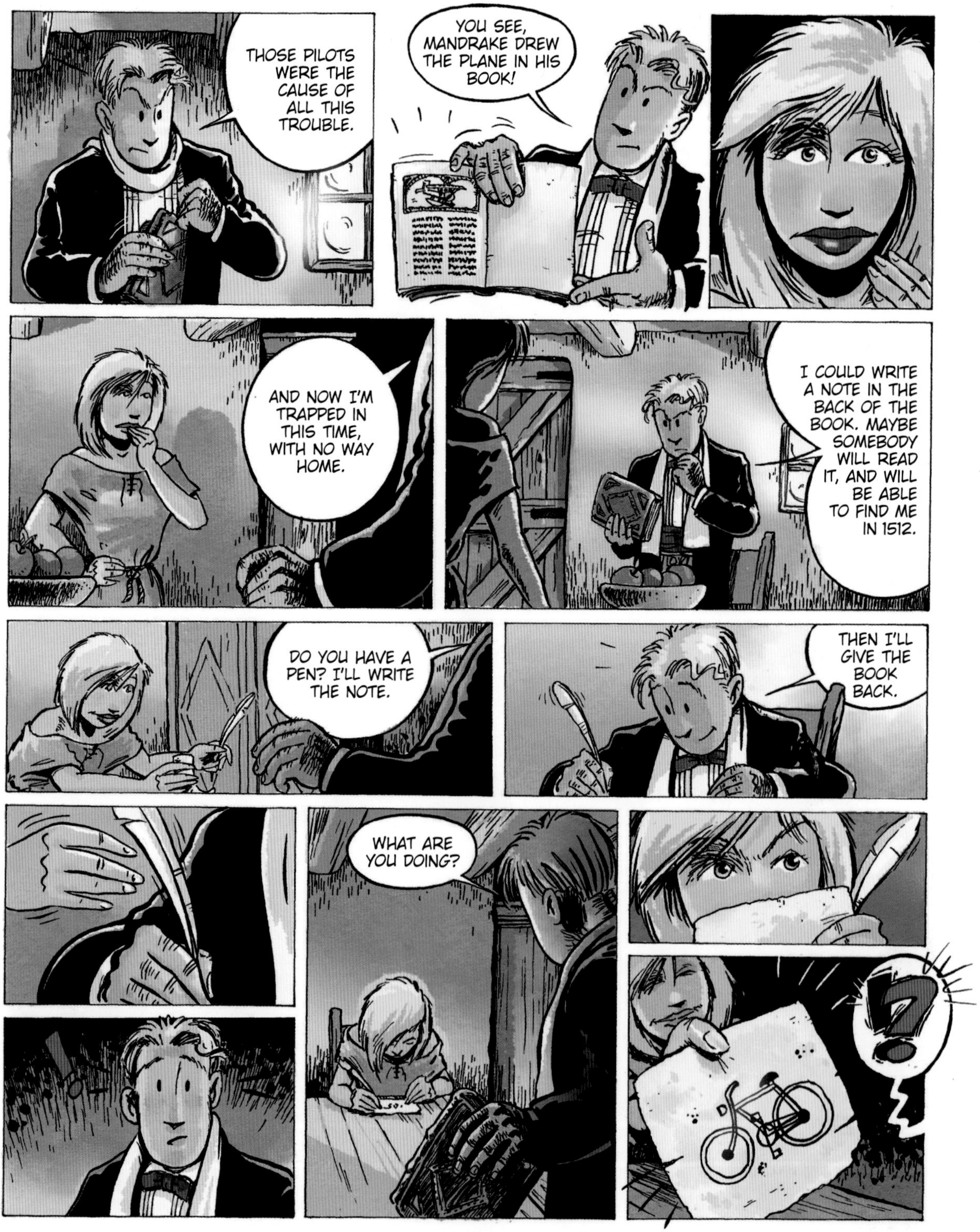
THOSE PILOTS WERE THE CAUSE OF ALL THIS TROUBLE.
YOU SEE, MANDRAKE DREW THE PLANE IN HIS BOOK!
AND NOW I'M TRAPPED IN THIS TIME, WITH NO WAY HOME.
I COULD WRITE A NOTE IN THE BACK OF THE BOOK. MAYBE SOMEBODY WILL READ IT, AND WILL BE ABLE TO FIND ME IN 1512.
DO YOU HAVE A PEN? I'LL WRITE THE NOTE.
THEN I'LL GIVE THE BOOK BACK.
WHAT ARE YOU DOING?

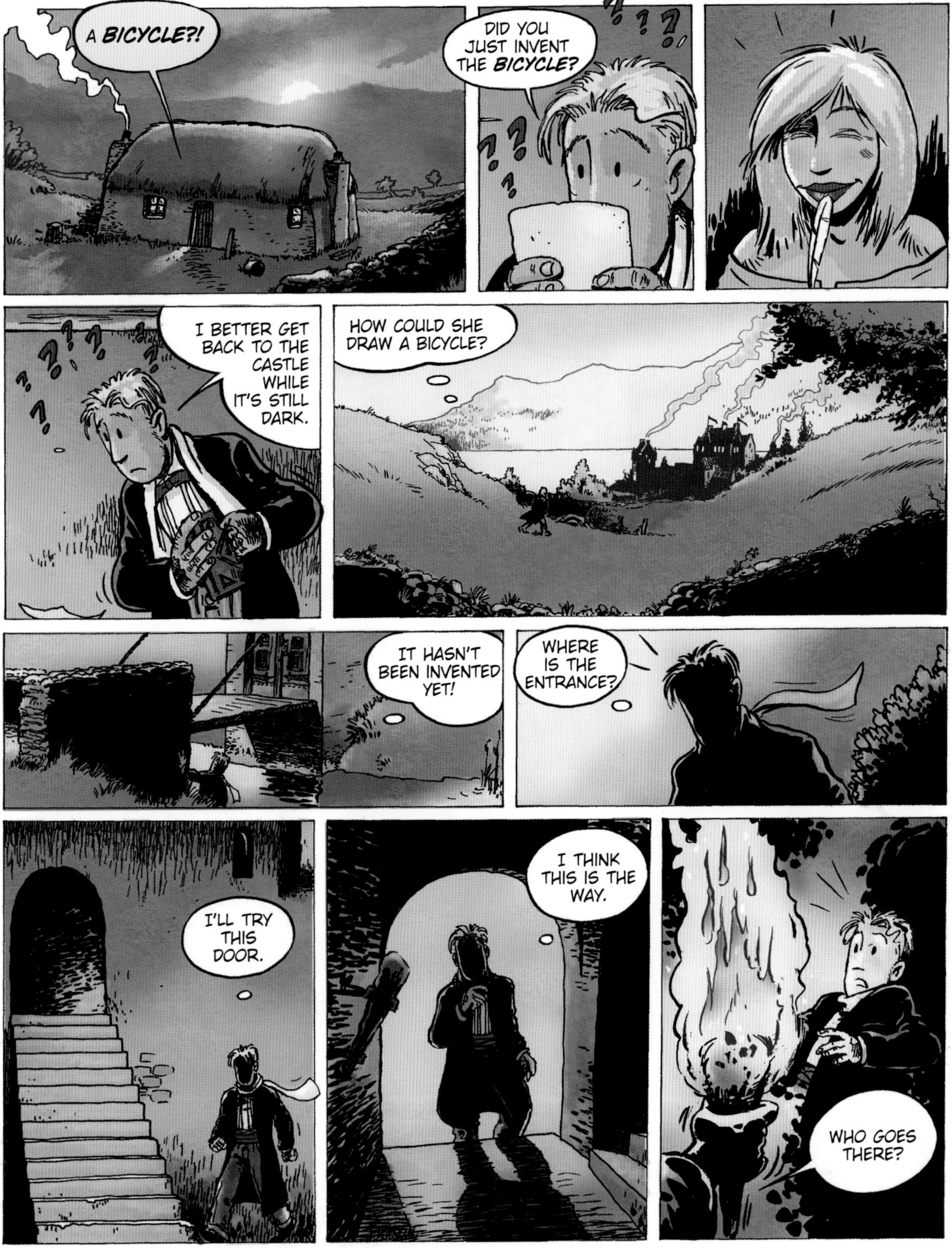
A BICYCLE?!
DID YOU JUST INVENT THE BICYCLE?
I BETTER GET BACK TO THE CASTLE WHILE IT'S STILL DARK.
HOW COULD SHE DRAW A BICYCLE?
IT HASN'T BEEN INVENTED YET!
WHERE IS THE ENTRANCE?
I'LL TRY THIS DOOR.
I THINK THIS IS THE WAY.
WHO GOES THERE?

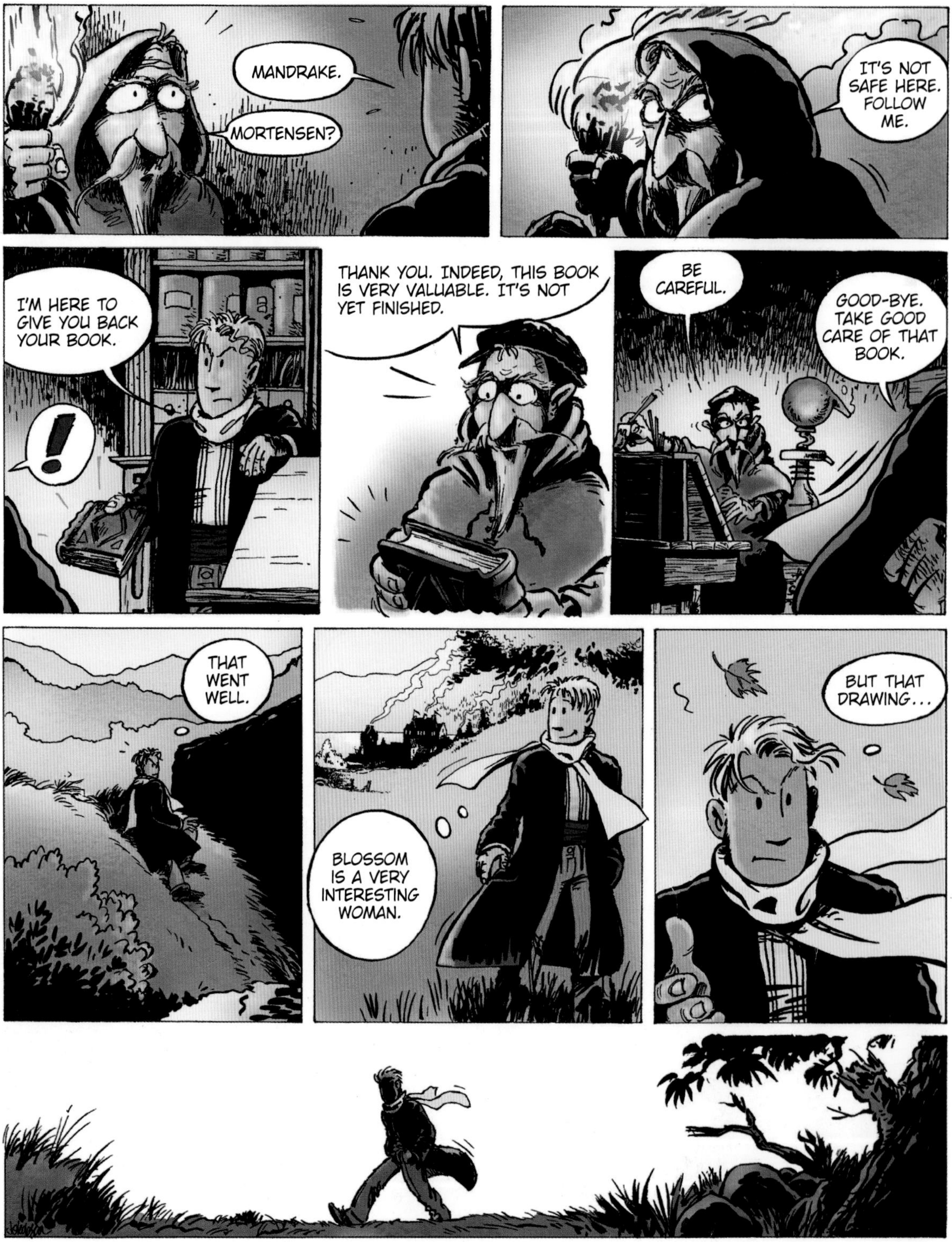
MANDRAKE.
MORTENSEN?
IT'S NOT SAFE HERE. FOLLOW ME.
I'M HERE TO GIVE YOU BACK YOUR BOOK.
!
THANK YOU. INDEED, THIS BOOK IS VERY VALUABLE. IT'S NOT YET FINISHED.
BE CAREFUL.
GOOD-BYE. TAKE GOOD CARE OF THAT BOOK.
THAT WENT WELL.
BLOSSOM IS A VERY INTERESTING WOMAN.
BUT THAT DRAWING...

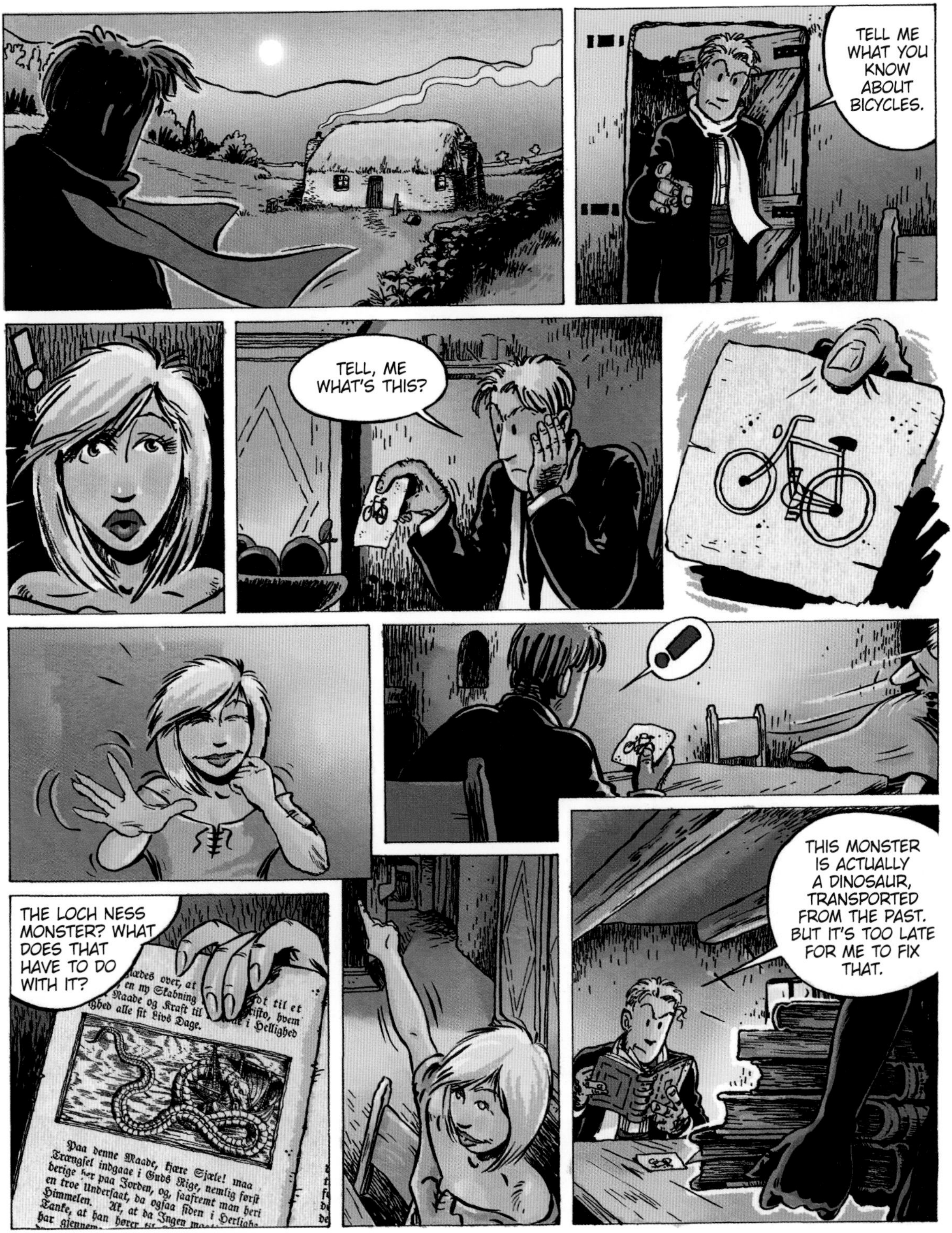
TELL ME WHAT YOU KNOW ABOUT BICYCLES.
TELL, ME WHAT'S THIS?
THE LOCH NESS MONSTER? WHAT DOES THAT HAVE TO DO WITH IT?
THIS MONSTER IS ACTUALLY A DINOSAUR, TRANSPORTED FROM THE PAST. BUT IT'S TOO LATE FOR ME TO FIX THAT.

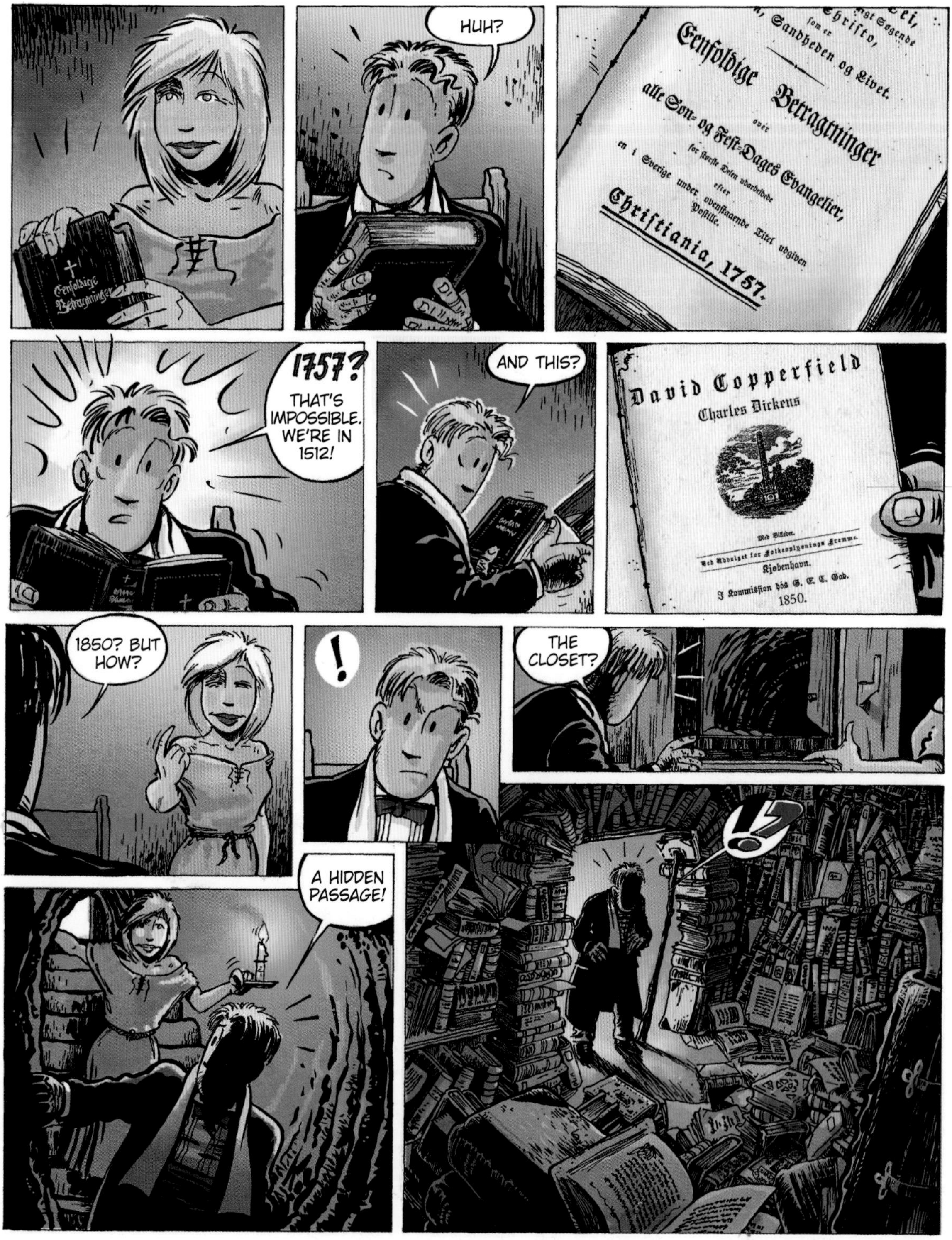
HUH?
Sandheden og Livet.
Eenfoldige Betragtninger
over
alle Søn- og Fest-Dages Evangelier,
Christiania, 1757.
1757?
THAT'S IMPOSSIBLE. WE'RE IN 1512!
AND THIS?
David Copperfield
Charles Dickens
Kjøbenhavn.
1850.
1850? BUT HOW?
!
THE CLOSET?
A HIDDEN PASSAGE!

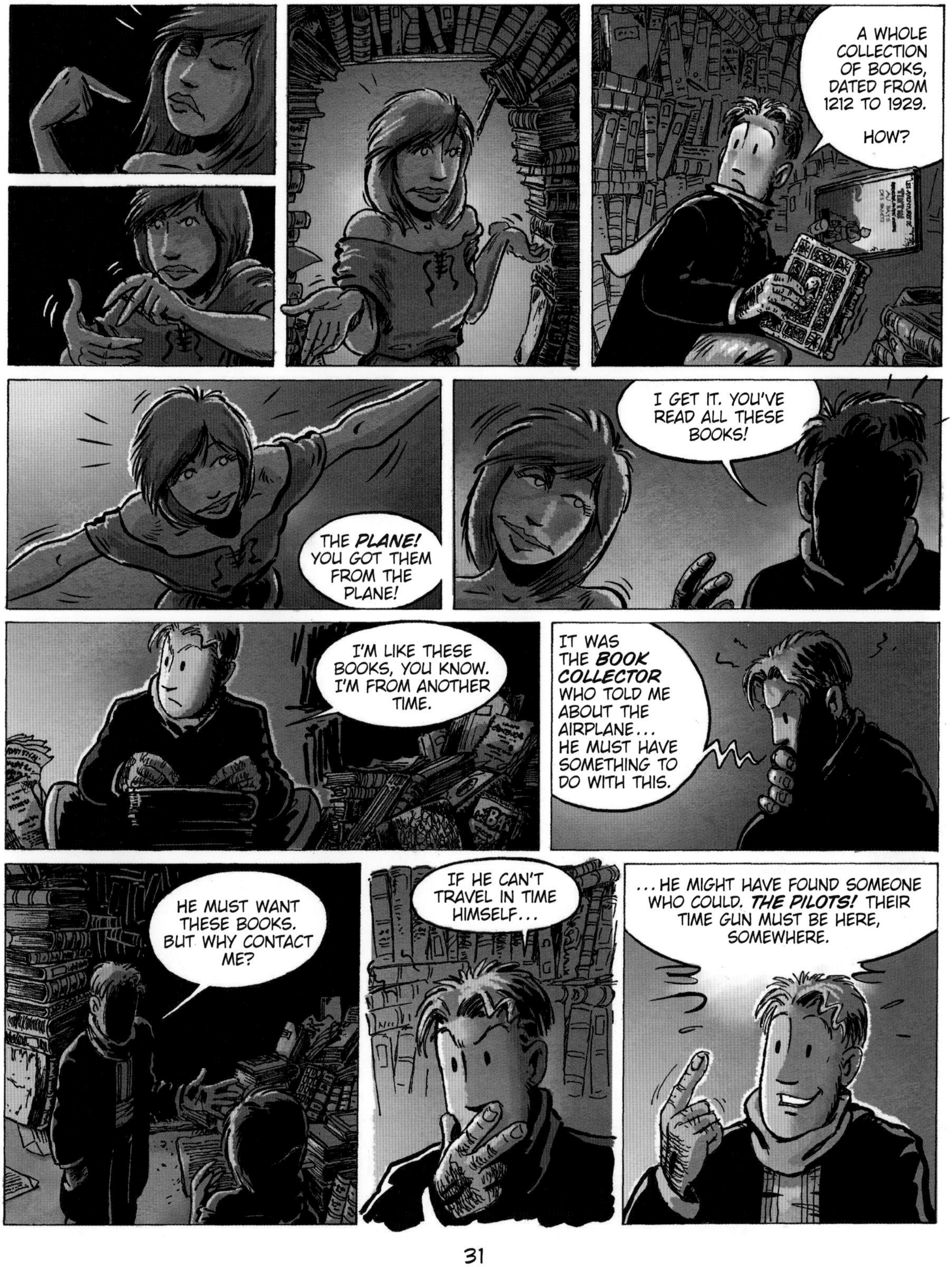
A WHOLE COLLECTION OF BOOKS, DATED FROM 1212 TO 1929.
HOW?
THE PLANE! YOU GOT THEM FROM THE PLANE!
I GET IT. YOU'VE READ ALL THESE BOOKS!
I'M LIKE THESE BOOKS, YOU KNOW. I'M FROM ANOTHER TIME.
IT WAS THE BOOK COLLECTOR WHO TOLD ME ABOUT THE AIRPLANE... HE MUST HAVE SOMETHING TO DO WITH THIS.
HE MUST WANT THESE BOOKS. BUT WHY CONTACT ME?
IF HE CAN'T TRAVEL IN TIME HIMSELF...
...HE MIGHT HAVE FOUND SOMEONE WHO COULD. THE PILOTS! THEIR TIME GUN MUST BE HERE, SOMEWHERE.

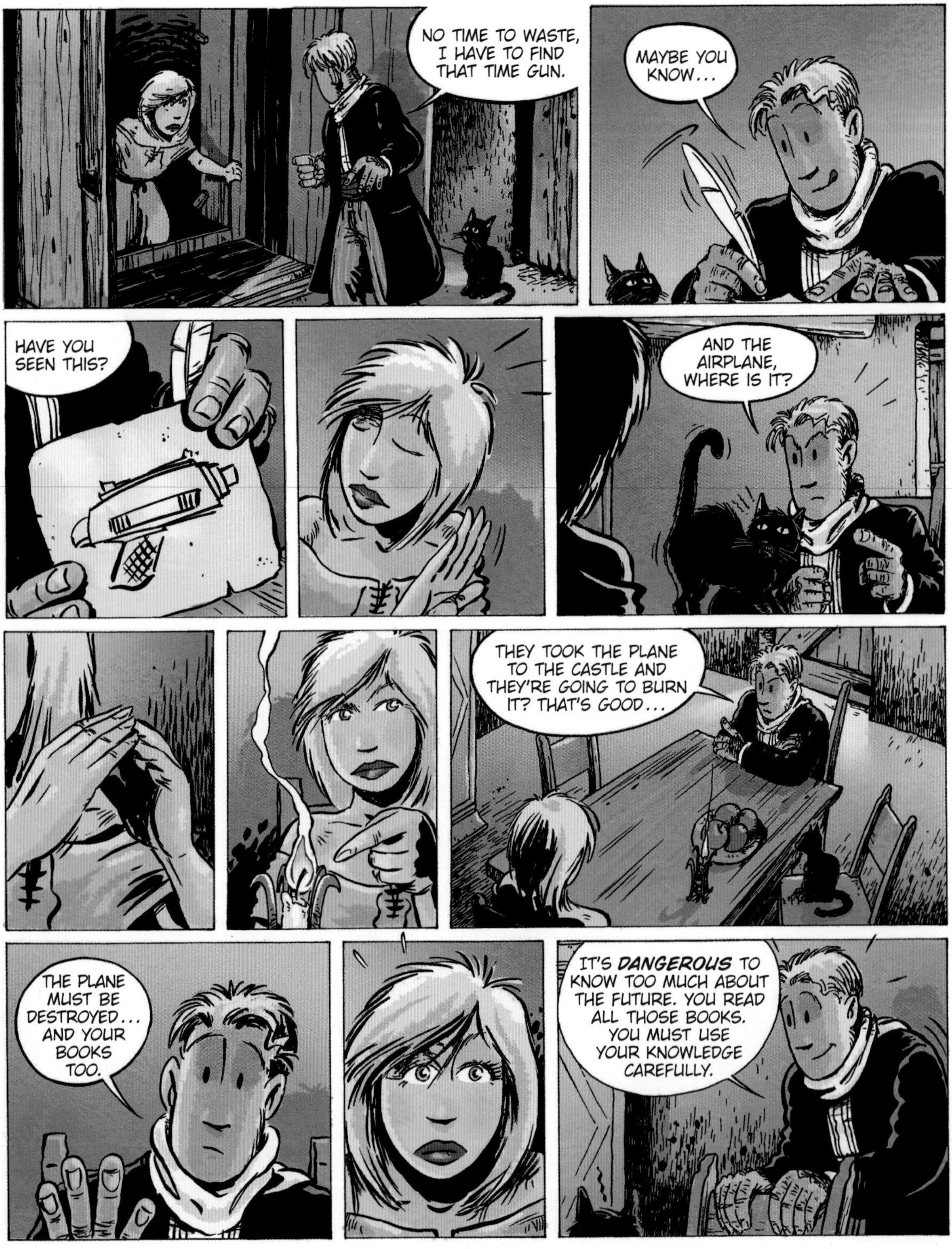
NO TIME TO WASTE, I HAVE TO FIND THAT TIME GUN.
MAYBE YOU KNOW...
HAVE YOU SEEN THIS?
AND THE AIRPLANE, WHERE IS IT?
THEY TOOK THE PLANE TO THE CASTLE AND THEY'RE GOING TO BURN IT? THAT'S GOOD...
THE PLANE MUST BE DESTROYED... AND YOUR BOOKS TOO.
IT'S **DANGEROUS** TO KNOW TOO MUCH ABOUT THE FUTURE. YOU READ ALL THOSE BOOKS. YOU MUST USE YOUR KNOWLEDGE CAREFULLY.

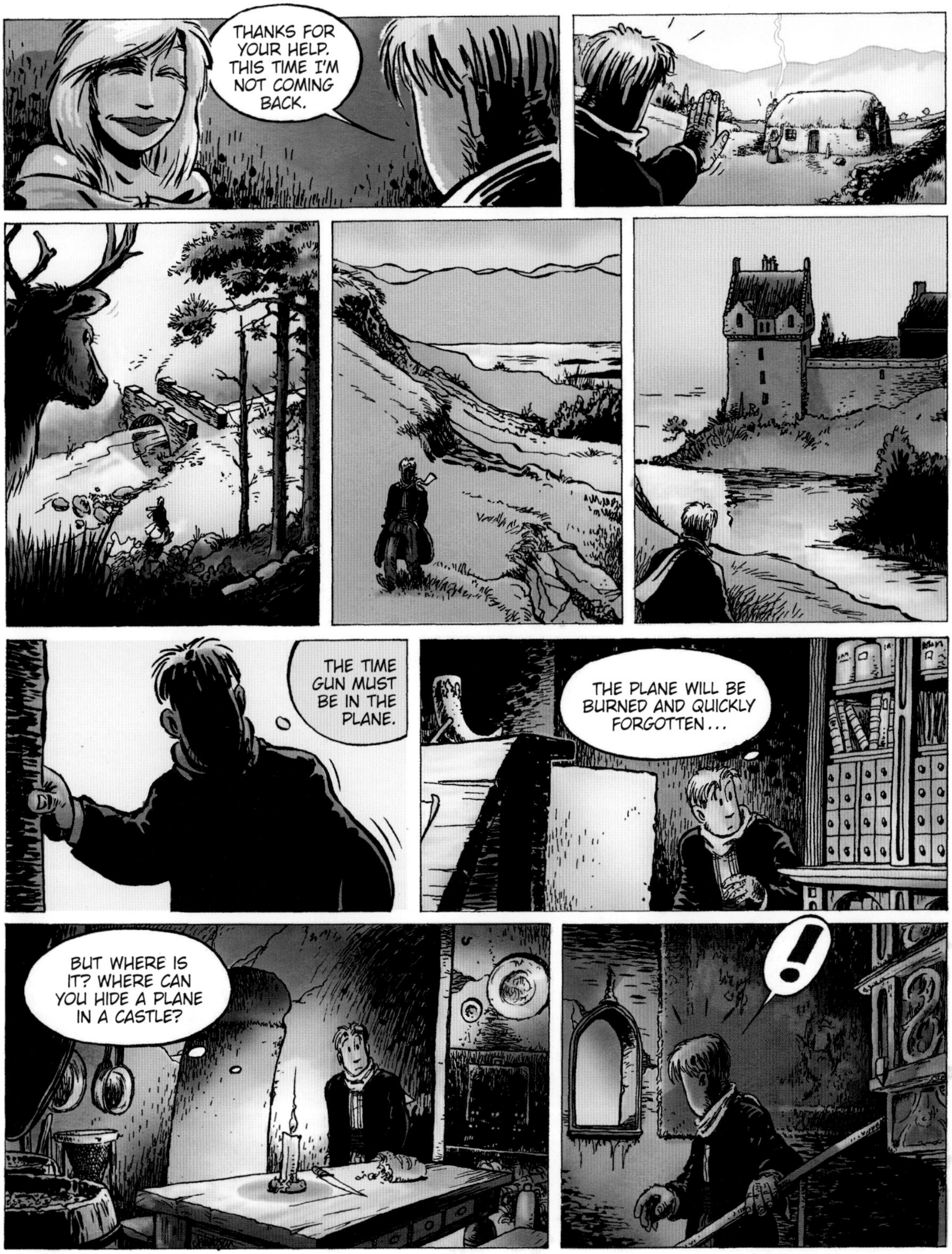
THANKS FOR YOUR HELP. THIS TIME I'M NOT COMING BACK.
THE TIME GUN MUST BE IN THE PLANE.
THE PLANE WILL BE BURNED AND QUICKLY FORGOTTEN...
BUT WHERE IS IT? WHERE CAN YOU HIDE A PLANE IN A CASTLE?
!

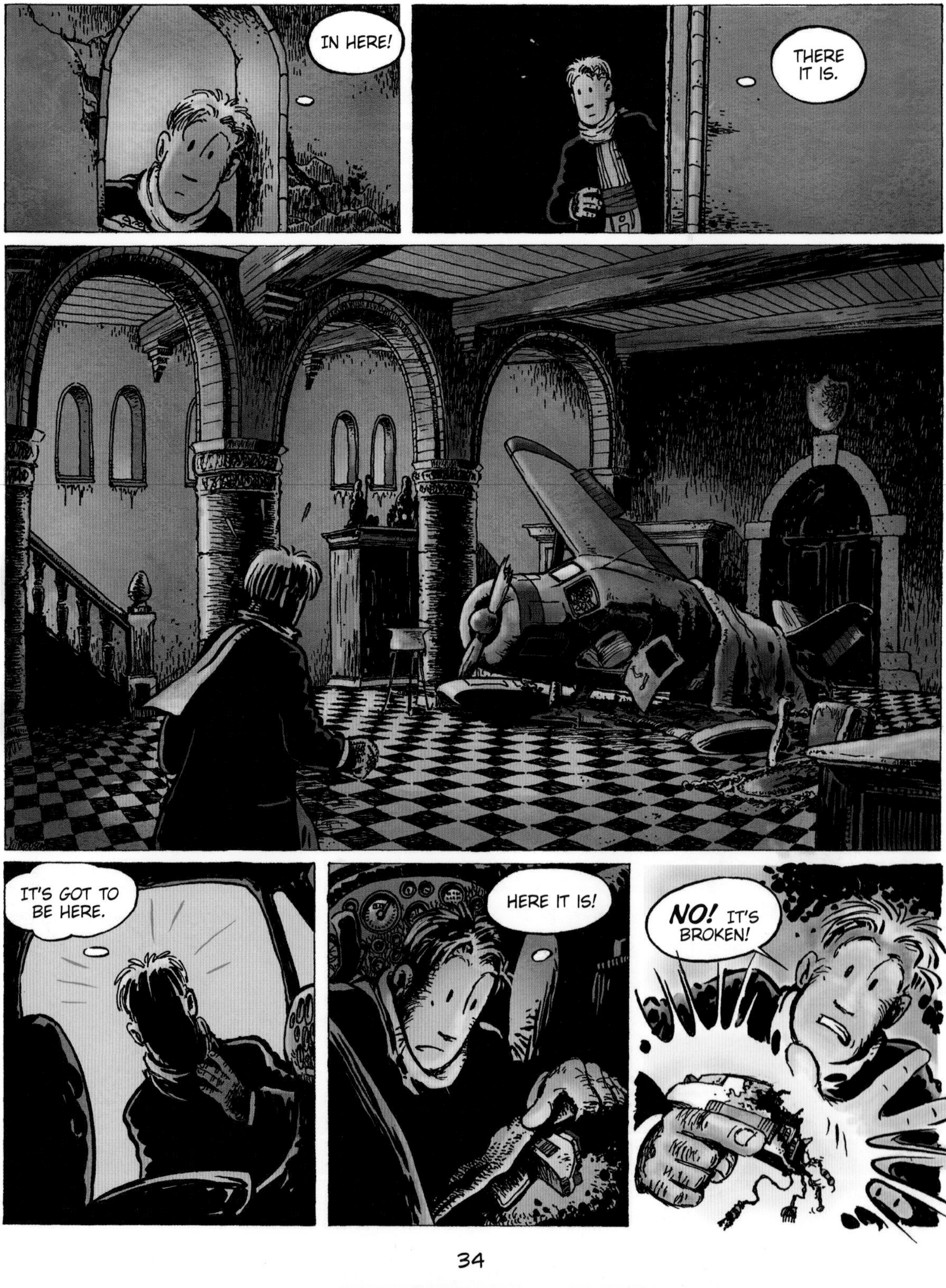
IN HERE!
THERE IT IS.
IT'S GOT TO BE HERE.
HERE IT IS!
NO! IT'S BROKEN!

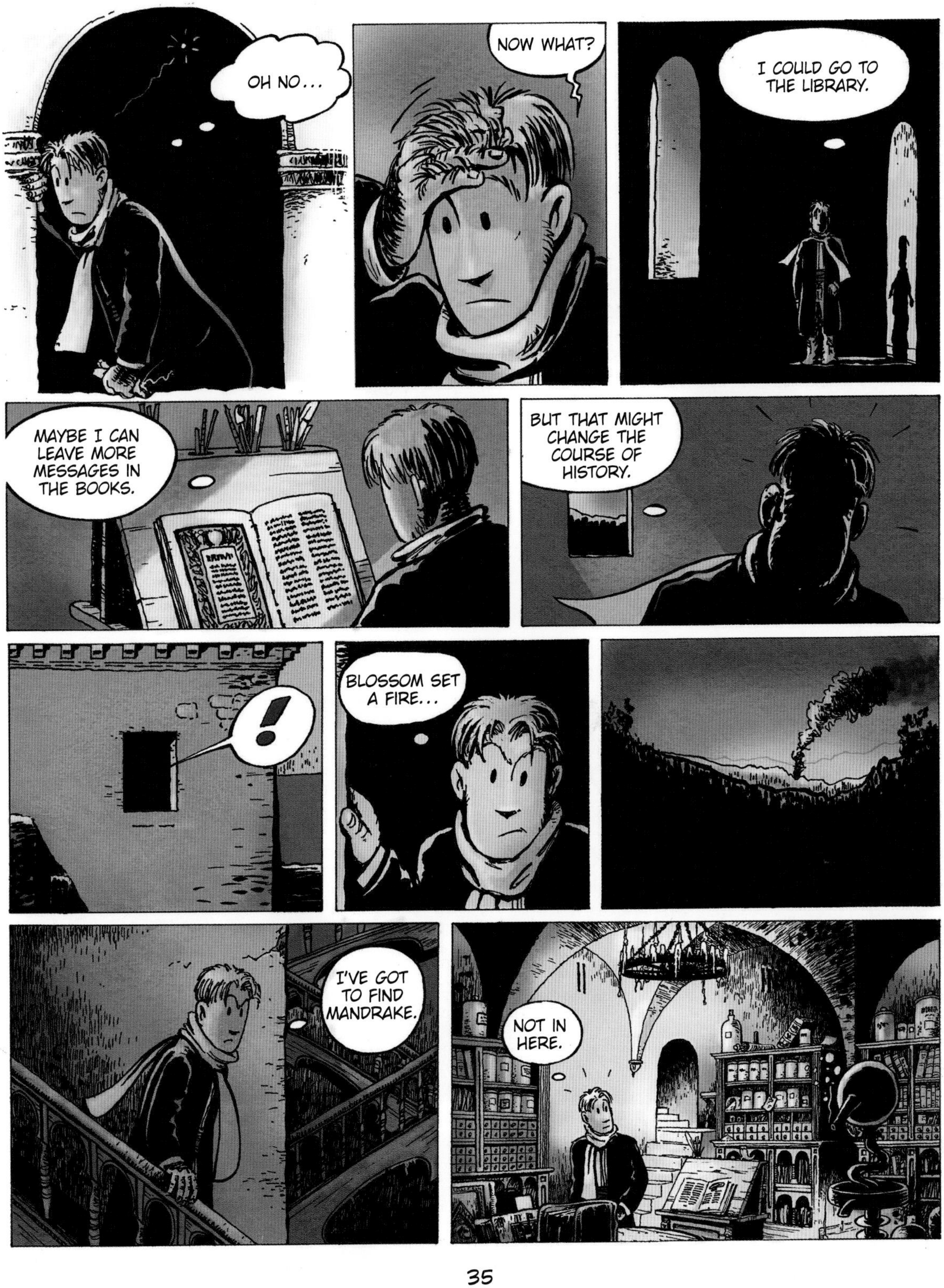
OH NO...
NOW WHAT?
I COULD GO TO THE LIBRARY.
MAYBE I CAN LEAVE MORE MESSAGES IN THE BOOKS.
BUT THAT MIGHT CHANGE THE COURSE OF HISTORY.
!
BLOSSOM SET A FIRE...
I'VE GOT TO FIND MANDRAKE.
NOT IN HERE.

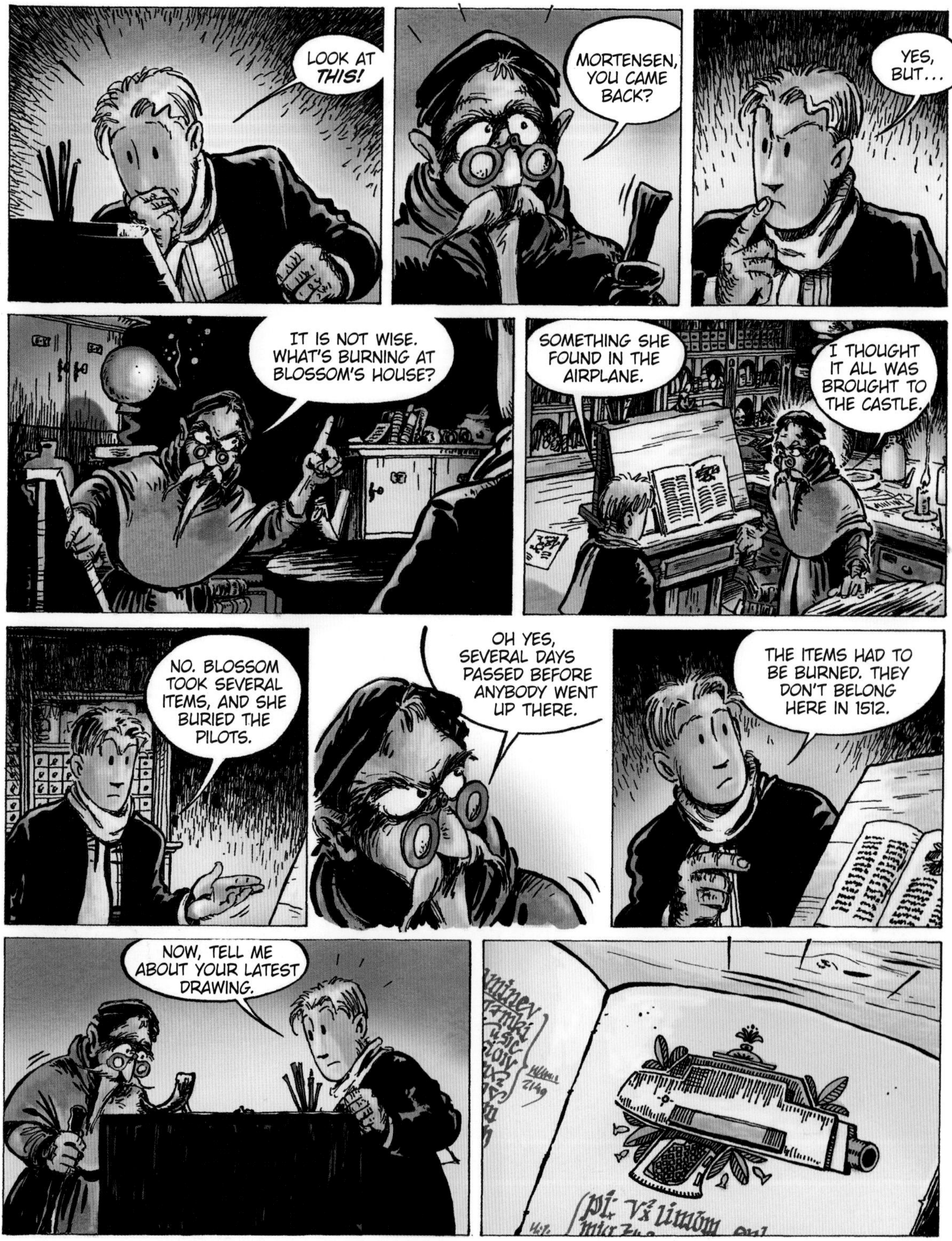

LOOK AT *THIS!*
MORTENSEN, YOU CAME BACK?
YES, BUT...
IT IS NOT WISE. WHAT'S BURNING AT BLOSSOM'S HOUSE?
SOMETHING SHE FOUND IN THE AIRPLANE.
I THOUGHT IT ALL WAS BROUGHT TO THE CASTLE.
NO. BLOSSOM TOOK SEVERAL ITEMS, AND SHE BURIED THE PILOTS.
OH YES, SEVERAL DAYS PASSED BEFORE ANYBODY WENT UP THERE.
THE ITEMS HAD TO BE BURNED. THEY DON'T BELONG HERE IN 1512.
NOW, TELL ME ABOUT YOUR LATEST DRAWING.

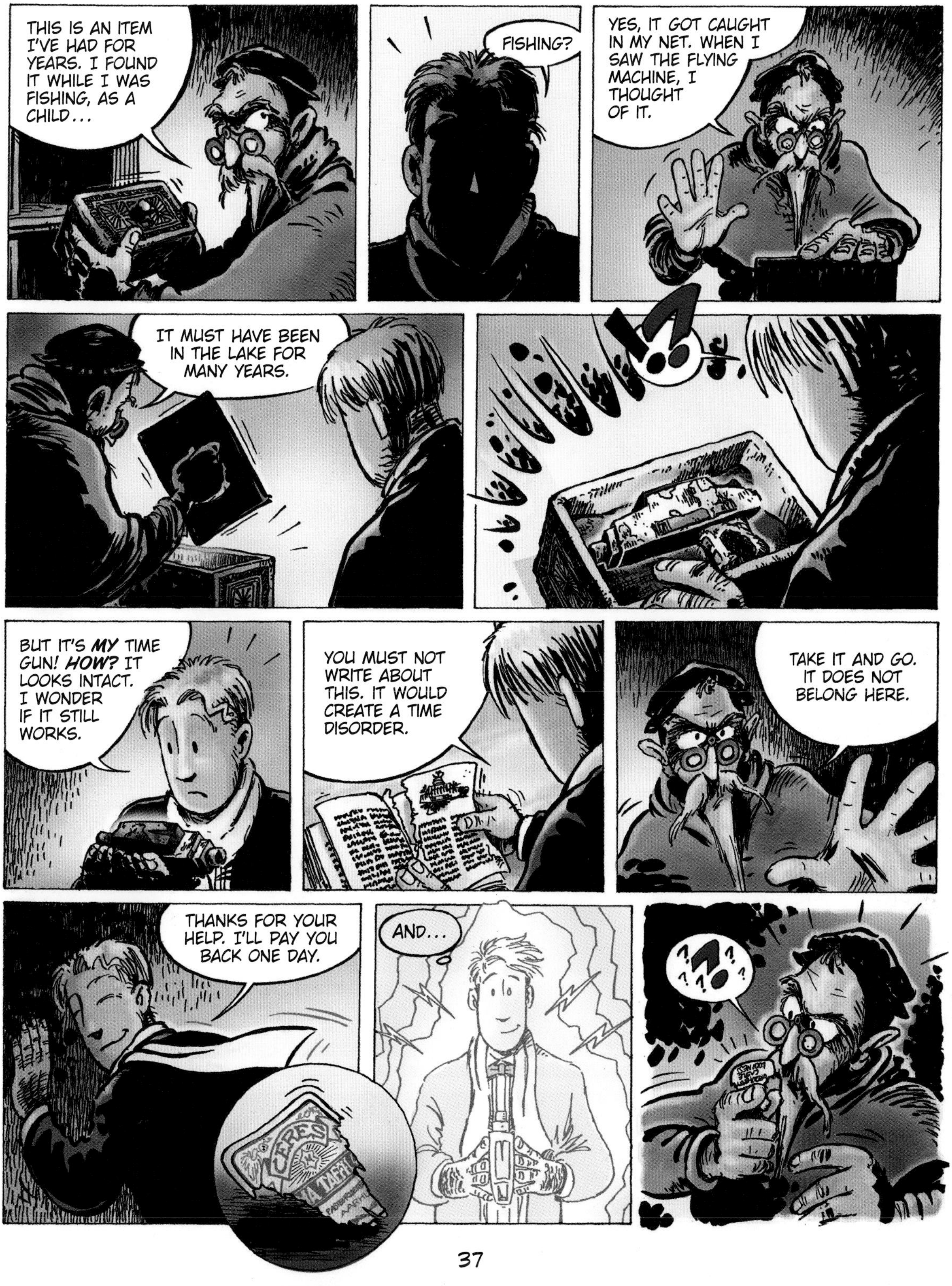

THIS IS AN ITEM I'VE HAD FOR YEARS. I FOUND IT WHILE I WAS FISHING, AS A CHILD...
FISHING?
YES, IT GOT CAUGHT IN MY NET. WHEN I SAW THE FLYING MACHINE, I THOUGHT OF IT.
IT MUST HAVE BEEN IN THE LAKE FOR MANY YEARS.
BUT IT'S MY TIME GUN! HOW? IT LOOKS INTACT. I WONDER IF IT STILL WORKS.
YOU MUST NOT WRITE ABOUT THIS. IT WOULD CREATE A TIME DISORDER.
TAKE IT AND GO. IT DOES NOT BELONG HERE.
THANKS FOR YOUR HELP. I'LL PAY YOU BACK ONE DAY.
AND...

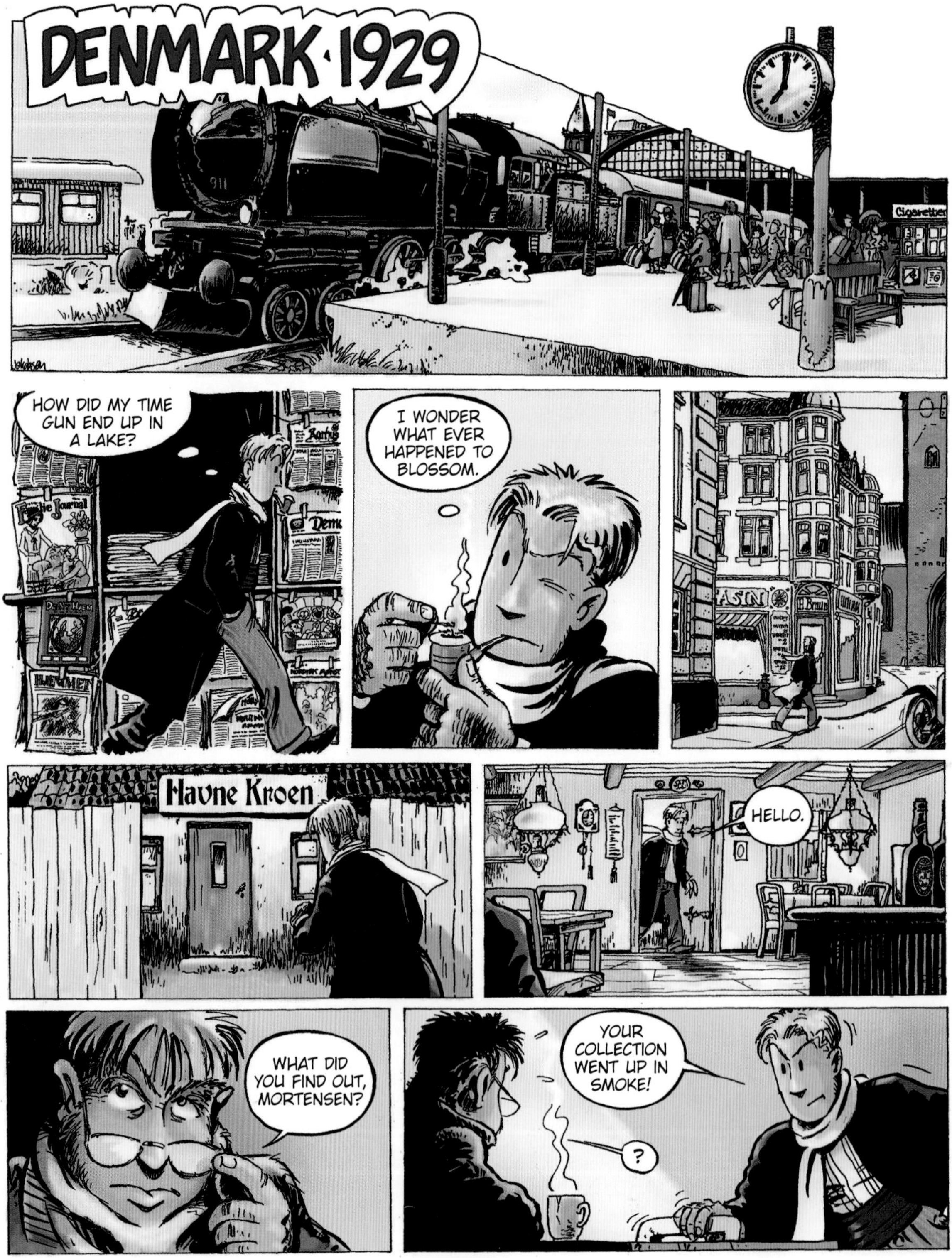
DENMARK·1929
Cigaretter
HOW DID MY TIME GUN END UP IN A LAKE?
I WONDER WHAT EVER HAPPENED TO BLOSSOM.
Havne Kroen
HELLO.
WHAT DID YOU FIND OUT, MORTENSEN?
YOUR COLLECTION WENT UP IN SMOKE!
?

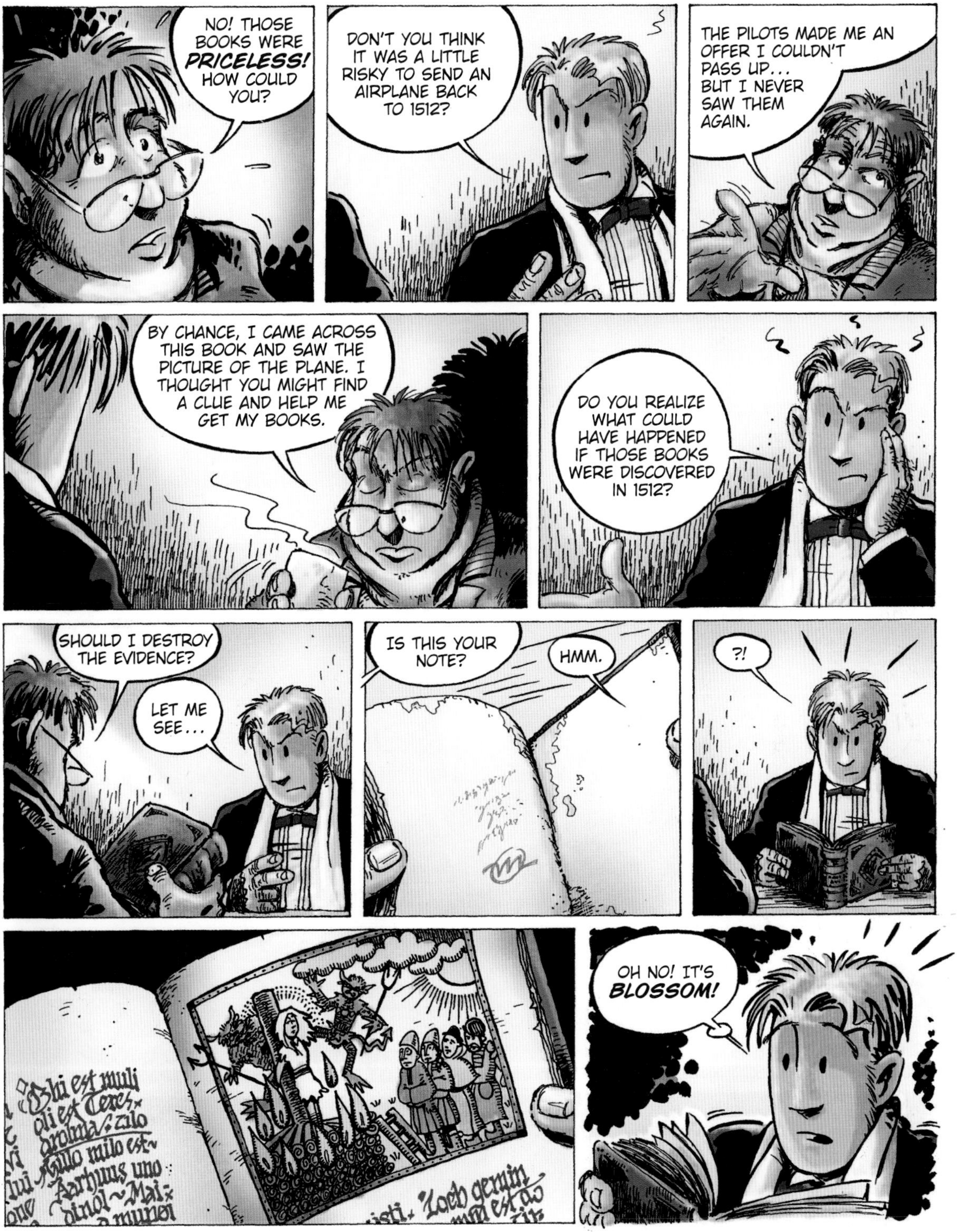
NO! THOSE BOOKS WERE **PRICELESS!** HOW COULD YOU?
DON'T YOU THINK IT WAS A LITTLE RISKY TO SEND AN AIRPLANE BACK TO 1512?
THE PILOTS MADE ME AN OFFER I COULDN'T PASS UP... BUT I NEVER SAW THEM AGAIN.
BY CHANCE, I CAME ACROSS THIS BOOK AND SAW THE PICTURE OF THE PLANE. I THOUGHT YOU MIGHT FIND A CLUE AND HELP ME GET MY BOOKS.
DO YOU REALIZE WHAT COULD HAVE HAPPENED IF THOSE BOOKS WERE DISCOVERED IN 1512?
SHOULD I DESTROY THE EVIDENCE?
LET ME SEE...
IS THIS YOUR NOTE?
HMM.
?!
OH NO! IT'S **BLOSSOM!**

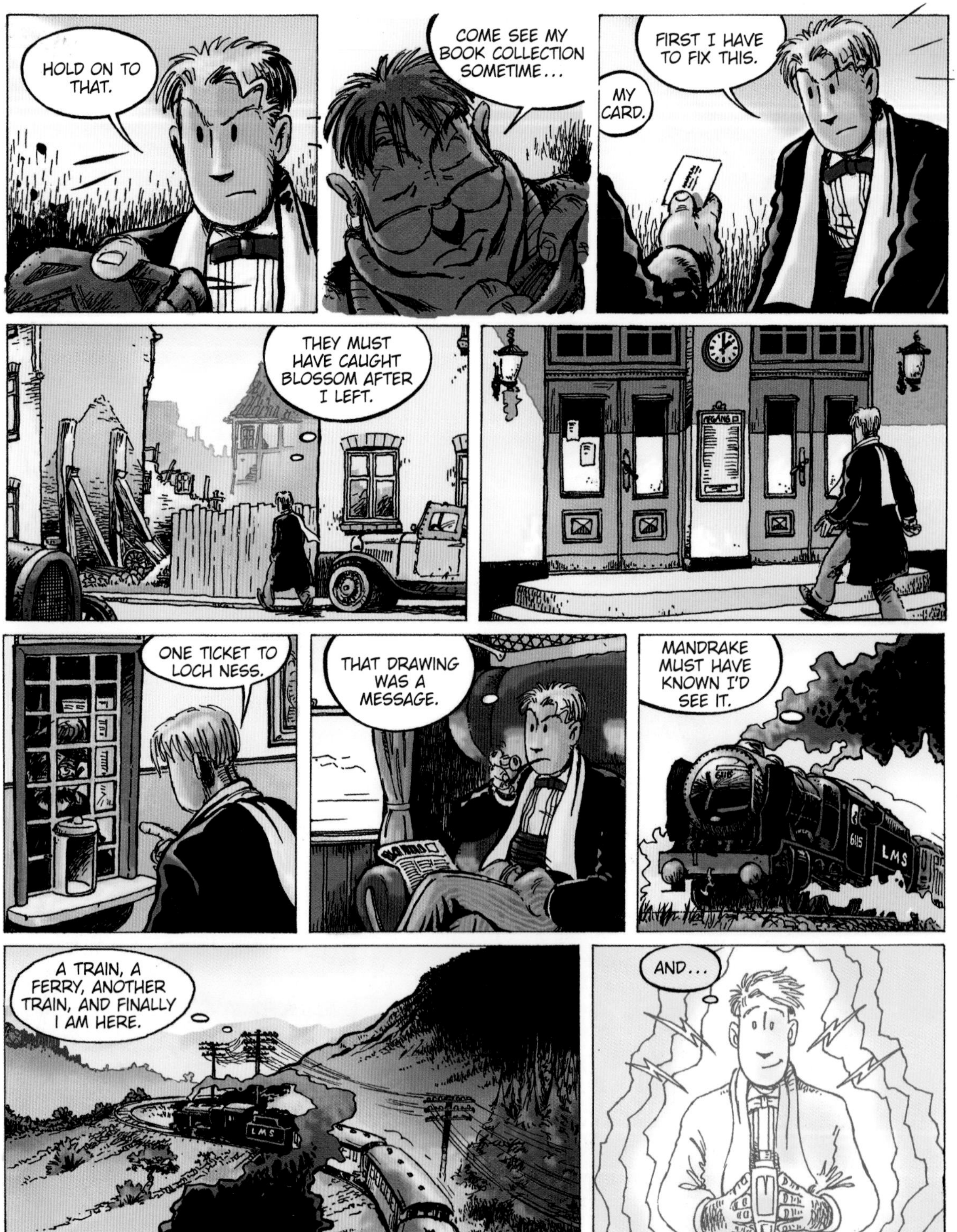
HOLD ON TO THAT.
COME SEE MY BOOK COLLECTION SOMETIME...
FIRST I HAVE TO FIX THIS.
MY CARD.
THEY MUST HAVE CAUGHT BLOSSOM AFTER I LEFT.
ONE TICKET TO LOCH NESS.
THAT DRAWING WAS A MESSAGE.
MANDRAKE MUST HAVE KNOWN I'D SEE IT.
6115
LMS
A TRAIN, A FERRY, ANOTHER TRAIN, AND FINALLY I AM HERE.
LMS
AND...

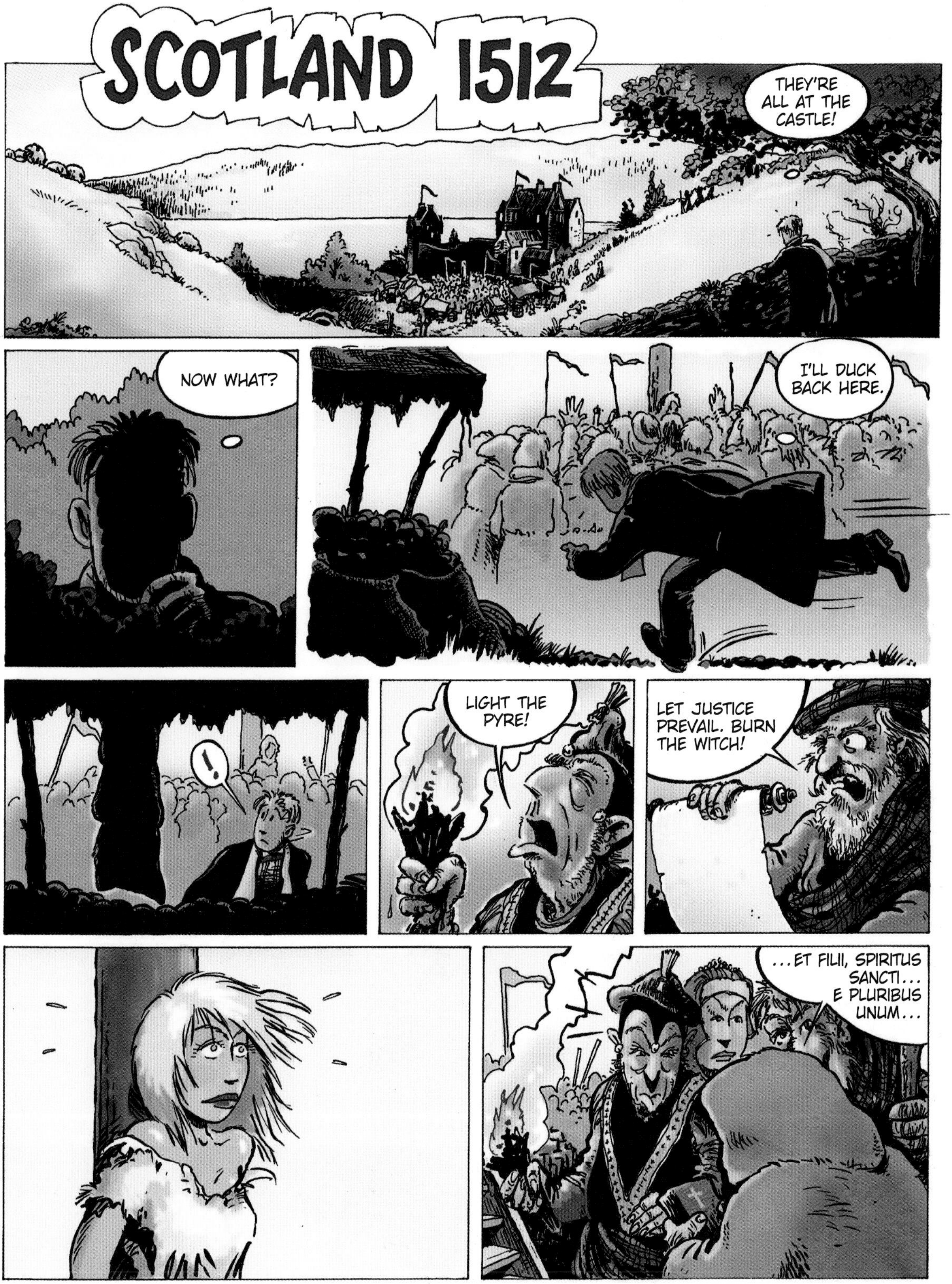
SCOTLAND 1512
THEY'RE ALL AT THE CASTLE!
NOW WHAT?
I'LL DUCK BACK HERE.
!
LIGHT THE PYRE!
LET JUSTICE PREVAIL. BURN THE WITCH!
...ET FILII, SPIRITUS SANCTI... E PLURIBUS UNUM...

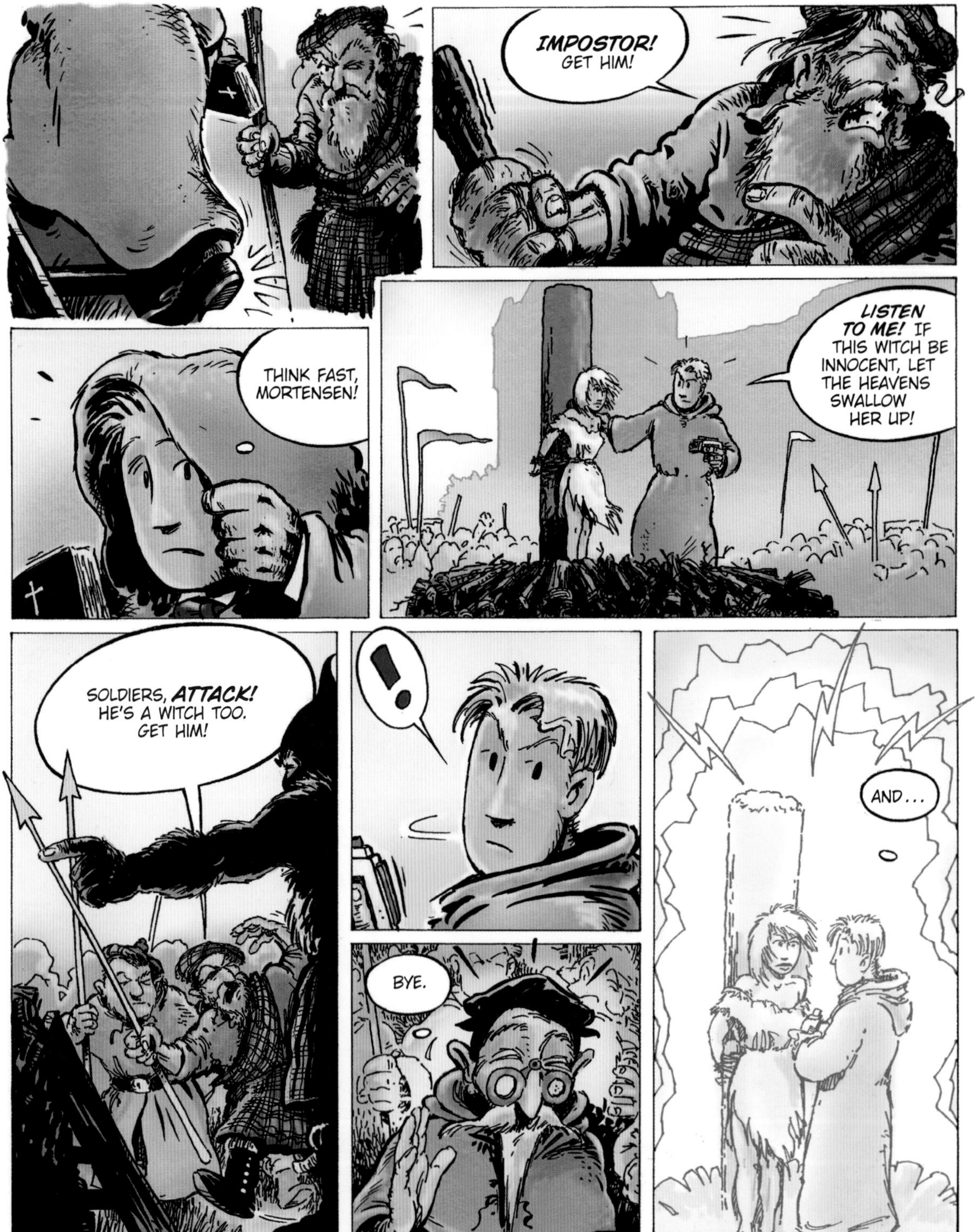
IMPOSTOR! GET HIM!
THINK FAST, MORTENSEN!
LISTEN TO ME! IF THIS WITCH BE INNOCENT, LET THE HEAVENS SWALLOW HER UP!
SOLDIERS, ATTACK! HE'S A WITCH TOO. GET HIM!
!
BYE.
AND...

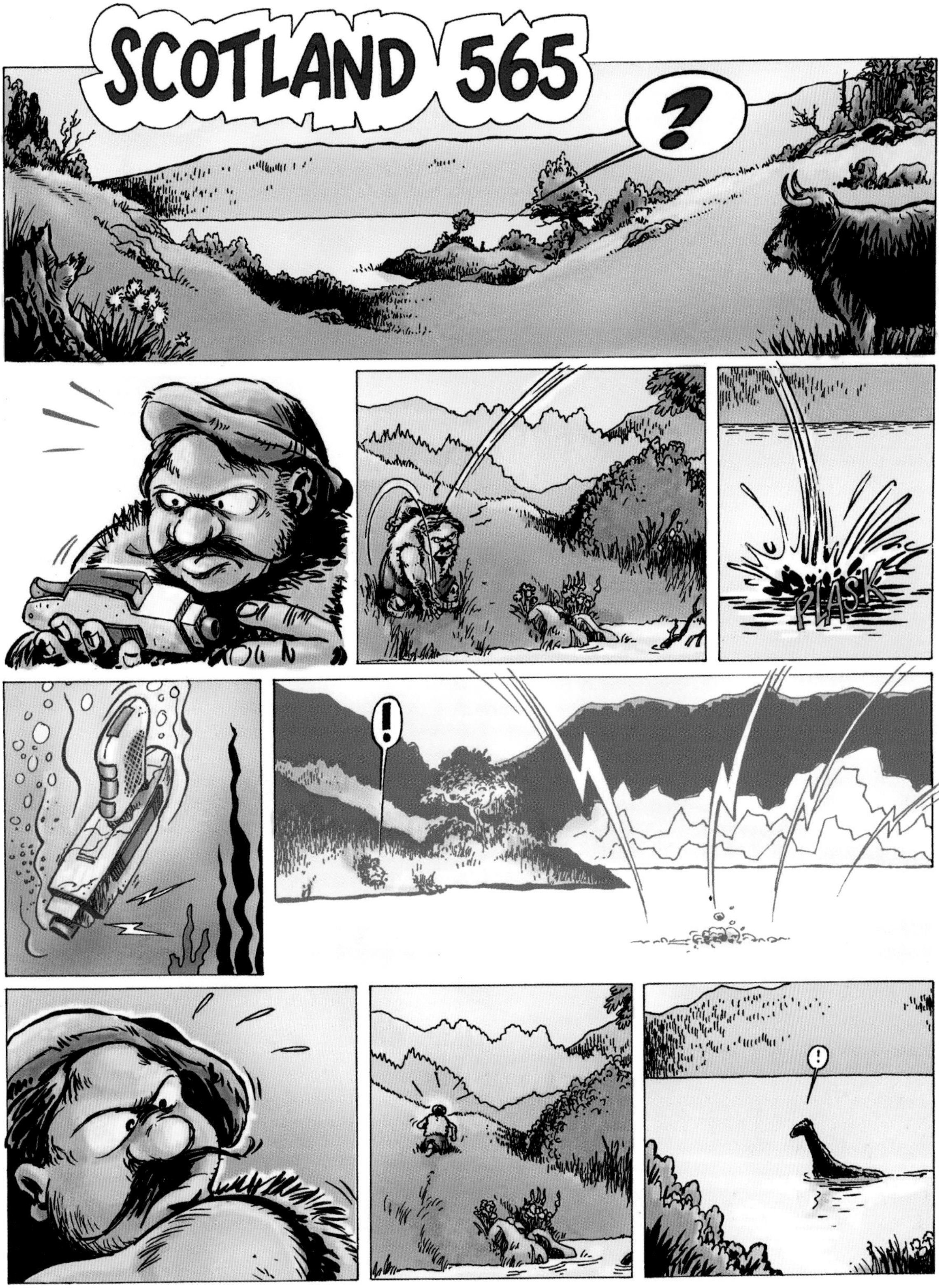
SCOTLAND 565
?
PLASK
!
!

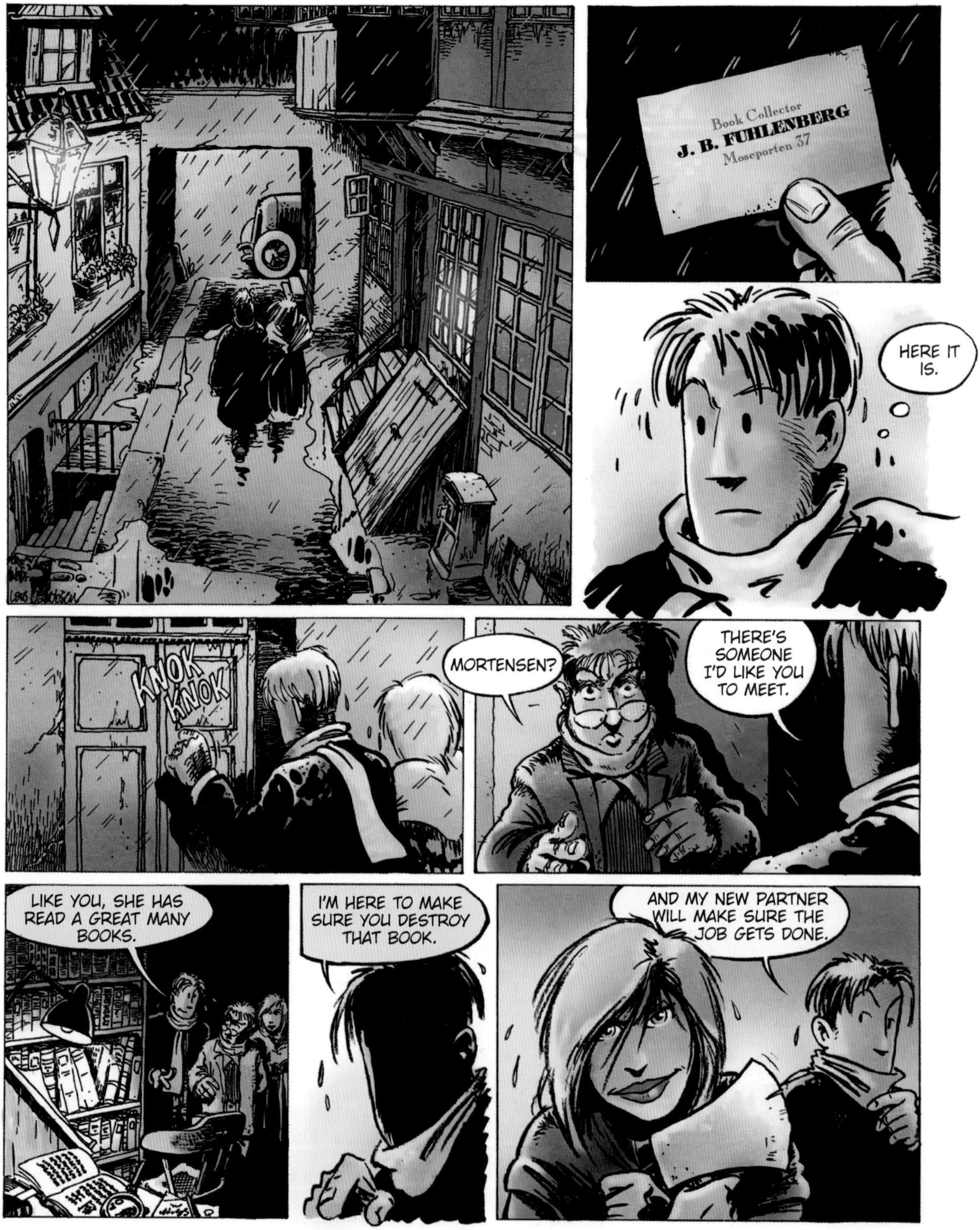
Book Collector
J. B. FUHLENBERG
Moseporten 37
HERE IT IS.
KNOK KNOK
MORTENSEN?
THERE'S SOMEONE I'D LIKE YOU TO MEET.
LIKE YOU, SHE HAS READ A GREAT MANY BOOKS.
I'M HERE TO MAKE SURE YOU DESTROY THAT BOOK.
AND MY NEW PARTNER WILL MAKE SURE THE JOB GETS DONE.

Illuminated Manuscripts

An illuminated manuscript is a handwritten book with pictures as well as words. These books were named for the silver and gold that often decorated them—they appeared to glow with illumination! Many of the illuminated manuscripts in museums today are from the Middle Ages, a period of European history that lasted from the fifth to the fifteenth century. While most medieval artifacts have been lost over the centuries, thousands of illuminated manuscripts still survive today. They offer us a record of both the art and literature of these long-ago times.

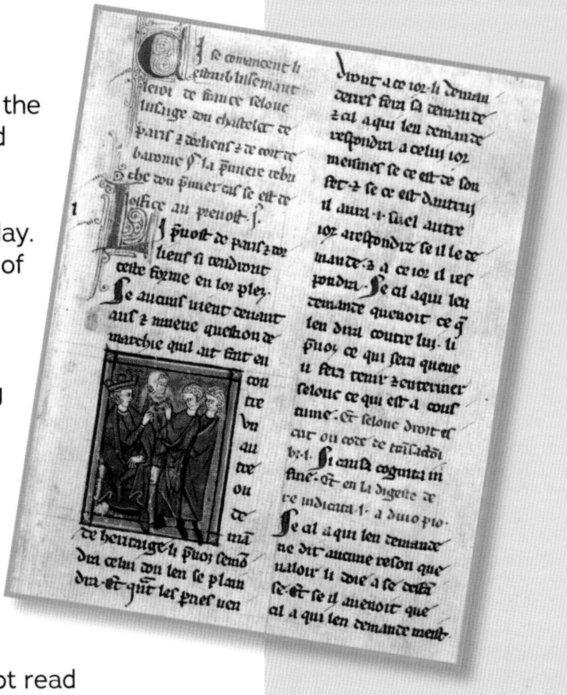

Most illuminated manuscripts were written on parchment, a thin material made from the skin of calves, sheep, or goats. A scribe wrote the text using a quill feather and ink. An illuminator decorated the pages with pigments made of animal, vegetable, and mineral ingredients.

Prior to the twelfth century most illuminated manuscripts were made by monks. As more universities opened in European cities, craftsmen began to produce manuscripts outside of the monastery. During this period, scribes like Mandrake were highly respected because most people could not read or write.

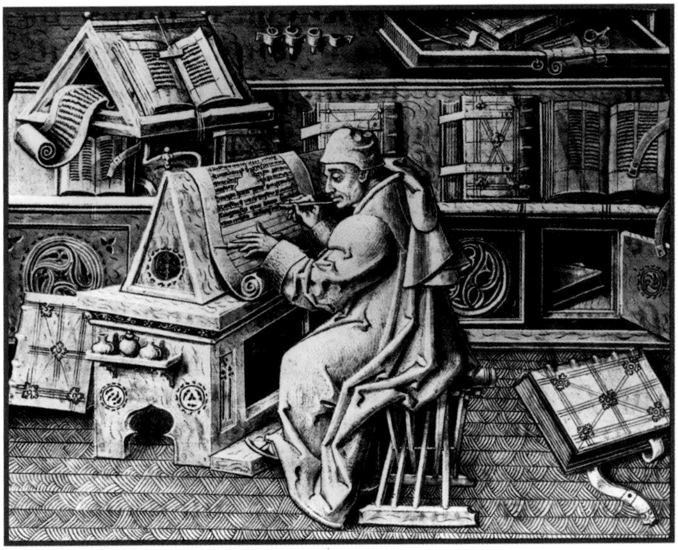

The First Bicycles

Not everyone agrees on when or where the first bicycle appeared. A German inventor named Baron Karl von Drais built a two-wheeled, rider-powered vehicle in the early 1800s. It looked like a modern bicycle, with one important difference: it had no pedals. Riders pushed their feet against the ground to move forward. Drais's invention was called the Laufmaschine (German for "running machine"), though it would be more commonly known as the velocipede.

By the 1840s, Scottish inventors had created a bicycle design closest to what modern riders use. Kirkpatrick Macmillan, a Scottish blacksmith, may have been the first person to build a bicycle with rear-wheel pedals. Another Scot, Thomas McCall, built a similar bicycle in the 1860s.

For a time, people thought that Leonardo da Vinci designed an early version of the bicycle. A sketch supposedly drawn by one of his former students shows a bicycle-like invention. A lot of people were convinced the sketch was the real deal, since Leonardo also drew designs for a flying machine centuries before the first airplane was built. He also drew sketches for a steam-powered cannon and a robotic knight! But scholars now believe the bicycle sketch is just a clever forgery.

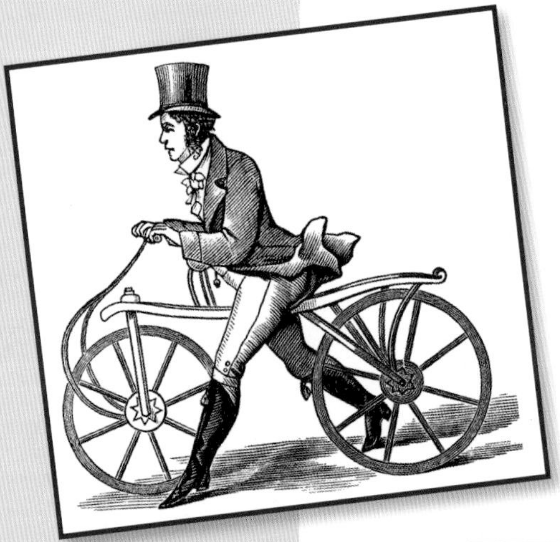

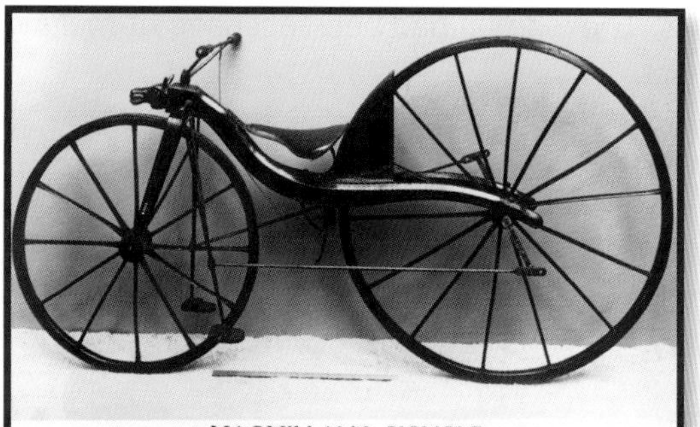

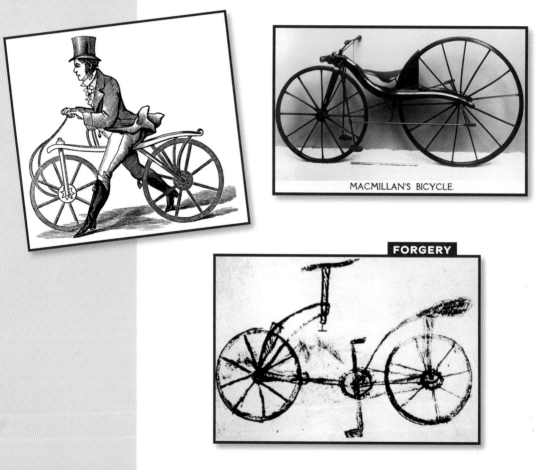

MACMILLAN'S BICYCLE.

FORGERY

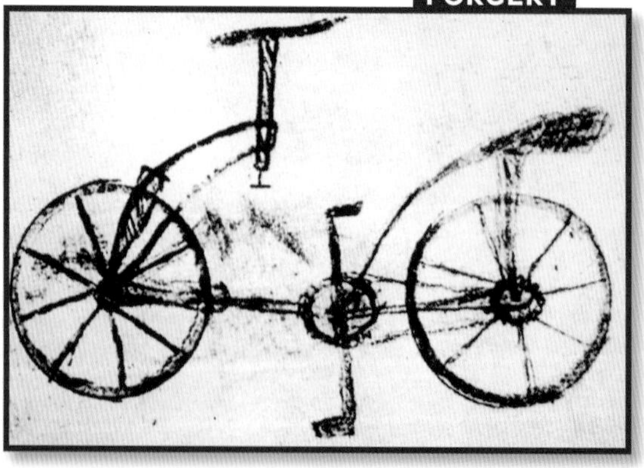

Witch Hunt

Witch hunts, or witch trials, spread across Europe in the 1500s and 1600s. Men and women accused one another of practicing magic and worshipping the devil. Nearly 2,000 trials took place in Scotland during this time. The most infamous Scottish witch hunts are known as the North Berwick trials (1590–1592). More than one hundred suspected witches were arrested in the town of North Berwick. Under torture, many of them confessed to performing witchcraft.

People in Scotland and elsewhere had feared witches for centuries. King Kenneth I of Scotland, who ruled in the 840s and 850s, passed a law that demanded witches be put to death. Under Kenneth's law, a group of women accused of witchcraft were burned at the stake in the town of Forres. The women had been accused of melting a wax statue of the king over a flame and causing him to become very ill. It is reported that the king returned to health after the witches were killed.

Dungeons

After he was captured, Mortensen landed in a dungeon—a common fate for captives in the 1500s. Accused criminals stayed in dank, dark cells while they waited for their trials. Most countries didn't use a dungeon stay as a long-term punishment until centuries later. When a person was found guilty, the actual punishment might be banishment from the country . . . or death. When it became more common to keep convicted criminals locked up for long-term punishments, the criminals were usually placed in larger prisons instead. But that didn't mean their rooms were any more comfortable than a dungeon cell.

The Libraries of Way Back When

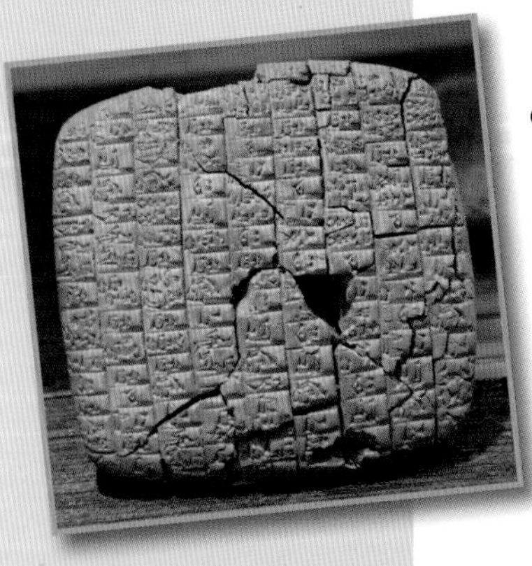

Where was the first library built? Hard to say. Libraries developed slowly, as the ways people told stories and stored information evolved. The oldest library yet discovered was in Syria, where archeologists have found rooms filled with clay tablets dating from more than 4,000 years ago. Ancient peoples used rooms such as these to keep records. Many tablets show drawings of livestock and document trade.

Some of the most famous early libraries stood in ancient Greece. Greek leaders and scholars created libraries that would have made Mortensen's book-collecting friend jealous. The city of Alexandria, on Egypt's northern coast, was home to a library larger than any that had come before it. Over centuries, scholars collected the best of the world's literature for the Library of Alexandria. At its height, it housed somewhere between 100,000 and 700,000 works. The library's huge collection of books was later reduced to ashes, though historians are unsure of how or when the fire that finally destroyed the library occurred.

In Europe in the Middle Ages, the largest libraries were found in monasteries or universities. The University of Oxford, in England, opened its first library in the 1300s. The library was located in a single room of a church. Work started on another library for the University of Oxford a few centuries later, and this one has become the second-largest library in England.

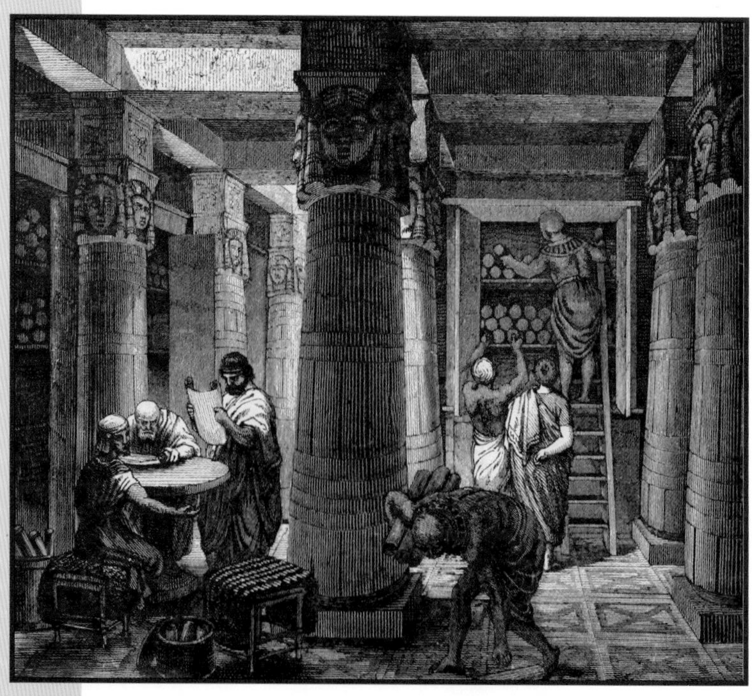

Story and art by Lars Jakobsen
Translation by Lars Jakobsen and Robyn Chapman

First American edition published in 2012 by Graphic Universe™.

Graphic Universe™
A division of Lerner Publishing Group, Inc.
241 First Avenue North
Minneapolis, MN 55401 U.S.A.

Website address: www.lernerbooks.com

The images in this book are used with the permission of: The Granger Collection, New York, pp. 45 (top), 46 (bottom); © Hulton Archive/Getty Images, p. 45 (bottom); © Heritage Images/CORBIS, p. 46 (top, left); © Hulton-Deutsch Collection/CORBIS, p. 46 (top, right); © English School/The Bridgeman Art Library/Getty Images, p. 47 (top); © Gianni Dagli Orti/The Art Archive at Art Resource, NY, p. 47 (bottom); © Peter Horree/Alamy, p. 48 (top); © Bettman/CORBIS, p. 48 (bottom).

Main body text set in CC Wild Words 7.5/8.
Typeface provided by Comicraft/Active Images.

Library of Congress Cataloging-in-Publication Data

Jakobsen, Lars, 1964–
    [Mystiske palæotyp. English]
    The mysterious manuscript / written and illustrated by Lars Jakobsen.
        p.   cm. — (Mortensen's escapades ; #1)
    Summary: In Scotland, when a mediaeval manuscript is discovered that contains drawings of airplanes, Mortimer Mortensen tries to find out where it came from as he fights irate Scotsmen, wrangles with a time paradox, and contends with an ax-wielding young witch named Blossom.
        ISBN: 978-0-7613-7883-9 (lib. bdg. : alk. paper)
        1. Graphic novels. [1. Graphic novels. 2. Time travel—Fiction. 3. Crime—Fiction.
    4. Scotland—Fiction.] I. Title.
    PZ7.7.J648My 2012
    741.5—dc23   2011027146

Manufactured in the United States of America
1 – CG – 7/15/12

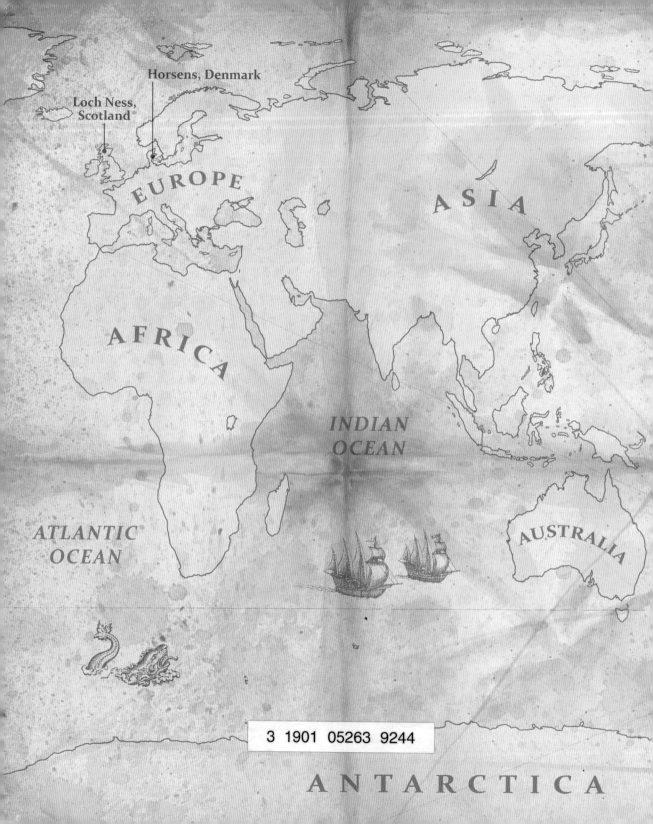

Loch Ness, Scotland

Horsens, Denmark

EUROPE

ASIA

AFRICA

INDIAN
OCEAN

ATLANTIC
OCEAN

AUSTRALIA

ANTARCTICA